The Castle of Creatures

Risvana Hyder

Ukiyoto Publishing

All global publishing rights are held by

Ukiyoto Publishing

Published in 2024

Content Copyright ©Risvana Hyder

ISBN 9789361724800

All rights reserved.

No part of this publication may be reproduced, transmitted, or stored in a retrieval system, in any form by any means, electronic, mechanical, photocopying, recording or otherwise, without the prior permission of the publisher.

The moral rights of the author have been asserted.

This is a work of fiction. Names, characters, businesses, places, events, locales, and incidents are either the products of the author's imagination or used in a fictitious manner. Any resemblance to actual persons, living or dead, or actual events is purely coincidental.

This book is sold subject to the condition that it shall not by way of trade or otherwise, be lent, resold, hired out or otherwise circulated, without the publisher's prior consent, in any form of binding or cover other than that in which it is published.

www.ukiyoto.com

To the souls like mine....

The Universe is the most powerful itself. It has a powerhouse called The Trio World. It's an integration of three worlds, named; The Magic world, The Peace World and The Dark World. They lived harmoniously. The Magic world has the purest and powerful magic. It is the most dignified world. The Peace world has light magic and it's the balance of actions of everything. Dark world uses shadow magic. It's the most fearful magic. But in the Dark world a group of people uses the evilest magic against the law of the universe. They use the sacrificial as the evilest magic known as The Dark Shadows.

Once the destruction by the Dark shadows spread all over the world immensely. By the sacrificial magic they became more powerful beyond the power of the Trio World. That's when the most powerful witch in the Trio World prophesied that the child of the Universe will be born into the magic world soon. She will become the Queen of The Universe. Also, in Trio World each child will be born to each world and one of them will become her king and others will be her companions. All together they will save the world.

"We're destined to find each other. So, I will find you again. Even if I have to set fire all over the world, even if it takes all the means, even if you hate me; I'll bring you back."

THERE'S A CASTLE
LIVING THROUGH THE BATTLE.
HOWLING FROM THE DEEPEST
FIGHTING AGAINST THE BLEAKEST.

NO ONE NEVER KNOW THE SECRET
LYING THERE'S THE STRONGEST;
THE ONES WHO HOLD THE WORLD.

IT'S THE CASTLE OF THE MIGHTIEST
ONE'S SHINIER THAN THE GOLDEN LIGHT
ONE'S STRONGER THAN THE MOON NIGHT
ONE'S PUREST TO BE A CLEAR BRIGHT
ONE'S BRAVEST TO BE A STRONG KNIGHT…...

IT'S THE CASTLE OF CREATURES
THE CASTLE OF CREATURES.

Contents

Let's Go Back!	1
Empty Home	3
Someone is Watching	5
Do We Know each other?	8
I Have You!	11
One of Us	14
Filling the Missing Parts	21
Hold on to Each Other	34
Shadows v\s Light	47
The Trio World	49
Destined Souls	56
Where All Went It Wrong	62
Broken Dreams	74
Different World	81
A Door to the Past Memories	89
I'm Home!	98
The Ones We Owe the Most	101
The Return of Darkness	109
Truth Behind the Lies	121
Retrieval of the Trio World	127
The Rise of the Unknown Spirit	133
The Rise of the Unknown Spirit-II	139
The Hidden Truths	145
Until We Meet Again	147
About the Author	*155*

Let's Go Back!

[Rustle of swords, noises, screams, magical voices, sparkles………..]

"No don't……please…." [screaming]

[Crying] "Don't die please…."

[Screaming] "Stefen…." [She startled from her sleep.]

"Did you see me in your dream again, Rya?"

He patted her head.

 "Stefen" she looked at him with her teary eyes.

"Guess like I'm." she replied.

"Come on, wake up and get ready. It's time to go. Uncle is waiting for us downstairs." Stefen said.

"Yeah, I'll be there soon." Rya said with a smile.

Stefen is a 21 years old young boy. He has White silver hair, ocean blue eyes and fair skin. He looks like a Silver Star in the sky.

Rya is a 19-year-old girl. She has golden shiny hair, golden crystal eyes, golden fair skin. She looks like the sun.

Rya is two years younger than Stefen. Even though Rya and Stefen are born from different parents; they're always lived as a real sibling from the day they were born. Their parents were best friends from high school. From that moment they all always lived together as a family. But when Rya and Stefen were too young their parents died. So, their parent's friend brought them into his hometown and raised them until now. But now they are leaving here and returning to their hometown. Their biggest wish is to study where their parents grew up, lived and fell in love. Now they came of age to go back and study in the Same University as their parents.

{Downstairs}

[Their uncle and his wife Mr. & Mrs. Rien and his son Shan are waiting for them. The servants were preparing the table for breakfast and some of them are taking care of the things for their journey.]

[On the dining]

"Are you two prepared to go?" Mr. Rein asked them.

"Yes." They answered while sitting on the chair.

"I've prepared your old house to stay as you wish. There will be a few more servants to take care of you." Uncle said.

"But uncle, we can take care of ourselves now. There's no need for so many people to take care of us now." Rya suggested.

"No, don't forget you two are royalty. Even your parents wish to live a normal life but when they have you, they want to give you the most beautiful life; that's why they built that home, they want to give you what you are worth. And about those people; they were honored to serve you two. So please respect that decision and honor your parents' wishes. Live as a royalty."

They were silent like there was nothing to say anymore. They just nodded.

"Please take care of yourself and have a safe journey. We'll visit you sometimes."

They sent them off. It's so heartbreaking for both of them. For Rya and Stefen they were the family from the day they lost their parents. At first, it's so hard for them to accept a new place and new family. But eventually they know how lucky they are to be taken care of by them. For my uncle's family they were so honored and dedicated to serve and take care of them, but eventually they took them as his own children. Somehow there were some special bonds that made this journey break their heart even though they were returning to their home as they wished for from the day they left.

'Goodbyes are always bittersweet.'

Empty Home

They reached their home by night. It was Dark already. They remembered the time they left their home; it's also in a night; the night they lost their parents. Until now they didn't come here even once. Now they are home after 14 years.

That mansion is at a lake area on the hill top, having beautiful trees and flowers around it. It looks so delicate. Roofs and walls are gold and silver with Black pillars.

Stefen held Rya's hand and he said "It's alright. I'm here."

After her parents died, Stefen is her world. He is like a parent to her. For him she is his only world too. He always believes to make her happy is the duty and responsibility of him as a big brother. That's why until today he always acts tough and holds his tears to give her courage.

"I know," she whispered. She is stumbling.

"This house feels so empty without them. It doesn't feel like home, but I'm glad that you're here with me brother. Thank you." Rya said.

"Yeah.... then let's make it a home. Our parents will be always watching over us. So, let's show them, the home they made for us is still a home. Even if it feels empty today, one day, we will call it a home again. That day this home is full of joy and happiness and my little princess's smile. What do you say?"

He patted her head. She knew he was trying to comfort her. She can feel his emptiness too.

"Then, that day, I'll say 'I'm Home!" She looked at him with soft eyes.

"It's getting late. Go and take a nap. We have to attend the orientation program at university and before that uncle said we have to meet the director. So please go and take a rest. Let's take a look at our home another time. Ok!"

She knew if they kept looking at home it would make them more miserable. And what he said was he wants to make her comfortable. And she was so tired too.

"Ok, then I will go and take a rest. You too do the same. Ok?"

"Yeah…"

[They choose to sleep that day in their own parent's room, so they don't feel alone.]

"Dad…. Mom…. I'm going to start my class at the same university as you." She sniffled.

"Uncle and auntie, I know you were always there for my parents, now Stefen is there for me… I'm grateful. I miss you all." she let her tears be a lullaby.

That day he couldn't sleep. He also let his tears fall down, so he'll get the courage to move forward and take care of her. He only lets his tears fall down when she is not around.

"I miss you all, but I promise; I'll take care of Rya and myself too. We'll be doing just great at our university. I'll not cry anymore and I'll not let her get hurt too. I'll be there for her anytime. I promise. So please watch over us, dad…. mom…. uncle and auntie…."

Someone is Watching

[Screaming] "No...."

She was startled from her sleep.

"Good morning, are you alright Princess...? Did you have a nightmare?" the maid asked.

"Yeah.... Good morning, I'm fine. It's kind of a daily routine now."

"Yeah, that's right." Stefen chuckled

"Good morning prince" maid greeted him.

"Good morning. But don't call me prince, call me Stefen." Stefen humbly said.

"Yeah, that goes for me too, call me Rya."

They get ready and they have their breakfast and get off as fast as they can.

[In the university]

There is a breeze welcoming them like it is waiting for them to come. They feel so refreshed and happy. They walk along through the ground looking around the university to find the office.

[Stefen's phone ringing......]

"It's uncle, let me take this call."

He took that call. "Ok uncle"

"He said, he will send me some documents regarding our entrance. So, I have to check it before we find the office." He said to Rya.

"Then I'll go ask them where the office is." She pointed some students a little far.

"Ok, but don't go too far." He spoke

She nodded.

[He is sitting on a bench near him, checking the documents.]

He feels so strange suddenly. Like someone is watching him. More than that it's a feeling he doesn't understand and yet at the same time he already knew. He looked around. No one's there. He turned his face and he suddenly startled.

"Sorry, did I scare you?" That young man asked.

He looks the same age as Stefen. He has yellowish-brown hair, ocean green eyes, and golden skin. He looks like a golden star in the sky.

Stefen couldn't say anything. His tears fell on their own. He felt something heavy in his chest. The one in front of him, who is he? He asked himself.

"I'm sorry. Please take care of yourself and take care of our little princess. You are not alone anymore. Thank you!" The one before him is also crying. Why is he crying, why did he tell me this? Did he know me and Rya? He asked himself. Before he asked him, he disappeared in the wind. It felt like a dream to him.

He looked for Rya.

[On the other side Rya]

After she asked the students about the office, while returning, she felt something strange too. It's like she has been watching. It's more like a wind. Because even when she looked around, she saw no one. But she was getting a feel that someone was watching over her, and she felt that it's not an enemy; but someone she cares about, someone she loves or someone she wishes to see. She felt uneasy. Her heart ached. Her eyes filled with tears.

"Rya, here you are!" Stefen appeared. He panicked, because he could see that she was worried. "What happened?"

"Nothing, I just felt someone was watching me."

He got confused. But he didn't want to worry her anymore. So, he just told her to let it go, it must be some stalkers. She tried to believe it even though she knew something was wrong about Stefen's too. So, she didn't want to make him more worried too.

"Are you done with the documents? I asked them where the office is, it's on the other side. Can we go now?" "Yeah, let's go." They walked to the office.

[In the office]

"Good morning, sir."

"Good morning, you must be Rya and Stefen. Mr. Rien called me earlier too. Everything is taken care of. Please show me the documents you have now. Then it's done."

"Thank you very much." They were so happy.

"We are honored to have you here!"

"No sir, the pleasure is ours." They replied to him.

They got out of the office. On the door they bumped someone.

"Sorry, are you alright?" Stefen asked

"Yeah, it's alright." That young man said.

When they raised their heads and looked at each other, they felt like there's a thread connecting through their heart.

Do We Know each other?

Rya stood there like a statue. She couldn't say anything. She felt a heavy pain in her heart, yet there's a feeling that she got back something precious to her. Her tears were falling down but she didn't understand why it was; is it regret, guilt or happiness? Even though, why? She just stood there looking in his eyes.

"Oh sorry, did I hurt you, is that why you are crying?" He panicked.

"No, I…. No, it's nothing." She wiped her tears.

"Do we know each other?" Stefen asked him.

"I don't think so. I'm new to this town." He replied while picking his papers and documents from the floor which were dropped from him when they were bumped.

"Let me help you." Stefen picked papers for him. "I don't know, I just felt that I knew you somehow. I'm Stefen. What's your name?"

"I'm Harry."

Harry is a 21-year-old young boy just like Stefen. He has night black hair; eyes are like black pearl and fair white skin. He looks like a moon at night.

When she heard his name, she felt something heavy in her heart. It's the same name she used to hear in her dreams.

"Do we know each other?" Rya asked suddenly.

"I don't know. I told you I'm new here. But I feel like I know you two too." Harry replied.

Stefen looked at her. He can see she is confused.

"It's ok, sometimes people feel like this. Maybe we're destined to know each other." Stefen said and smiled. "Yeah, you think so?" Harry smiled at him. "So which departments are you enrolled in? Harry asked.

"Ooh, I'm in the business arts senior section. What about you?" Stefen asked.

"Oh, that's great. I'm too." When Harry said that they both were so happy, it's like two best friends who don't want to separate and enrolled into the same class.

"What about you? What's your name?" Harry looked at Rya and asked. He can see she is still so confused.

"I'm Rya. I'm in business arts too, but in the junior section." She spoke.

"This is my little sister." Stefen patted her head.

"So, what are you doing at the office door?" Stefen asked Harry.

"Oh no, I was in a hurry to see the director, but I forgot. I have to give him these documents." Harry panicked.

"Then you go and give him that, we'll wait here. Let's go back together, brother!" Stefen said.

When Stefen called him brother, Harry cried with a smile. He couldn't hold back his tears. He hugged Stefen. When he hugged him, Stefen was crying too. He just felt that what he said was true, maybe that they were destined to know each other.

Rya was also shocked. Because in her life she never heard Stefen calling someone brother, even if they were living with their uncle's son Stefen never mentioned him brother. But now Stefen called someone brother and they were hugging like long lost brothers. She looked at them with adore.

[Later]

They had their first day in their university. They were in the garden area having their funds and chats. After that they said goodbye to each other.

Time passed. Even though so many questions remain in their mind, they become more attached to each other. They were always together.

It's the first time Rya and Stefen let anyone enter into their life like this. They never let anyone come into their world. Stefen keeps calling Harry 'brother' and so does Harry. Even though Rya felt conflict in her heart, she loves Harry's presence.

Being in pain and joy in her heart, she knew he was someone she knew already. Not in just dreams but something more than that. She knows he is someone she loves. But, why is it? That always remained in her mind.

I Have You!

[On a brighter day; Stefen and Rya sitting on a bench in the faculty ground waiting for Harry. Stefen is reading a book and Rya put her head on Stefen's shoulder.]

"It's a beautiful day, isn't it?" Rya asked.

"Yeah, it is. Just like me." Stefen looked at the sky and replied.

"Stefen, can I ask you something?" Rya asked.

"Yes, of course. Why so formal? Do you want to know why I'm so beautiful? Is that what you're thinking? Well, you know I'm just born like this. Tell me, I just look so cool while reading this book here, isn't it?" Stefen laughed.

"You'll never get tired of this, do you? Huh.... forget it. I don't care to ask you anymore." Rya sighed.

Stefen laughed. "Come on. Don't be jealous of your own brother. You also inherit my beauty. So don't worry, go on, ask what you want." Stefen chuckled.

Rya sighed and smiled. She is happy to see his smile. "You're really insane, idiot."

Stefen laughed and said "come on, ask!"

"Why are you always calling Harry 'brother'? Even though we live with Shan, I never heard you call him brother. Then why call him." She looked at Stefen.

"In fact, I don't really know that either. Even I wondered why, but I don't have an answer. You know when the first time we met him, I just felt that I got back my lost brother. It doesn't have a reason. When we lived with Shan, I considered him as a family. But I don't feel like he is my friend or a brother or anything. You know, I really don't talk to him. I never want to share with him my worries, thoughts or even my happiness. But with Harry, he is my best friend now. More than that, he is my own brother. It's what it is. Maybe in previous life we were really best buddies or we're real sworn brothers. What do you think?" Stefen said to her.

"Previous life, it is nonsense. But I'll tell you something, I really envy your friendship. But I don't want to share it with you. You are my brother. Do you get it?" Rya pouted.

Stefen laughed. "Then let me ask you something too? You never let anyone come into your life either. Then why is it, Harry? Is it love? Do you like him?" Stefen asked and looked at her.

She was too stunned. She wants to give an answer to him, but before that she wants to give an answer to herself.

"What are you guys doing?" Harry appeared. "Oh, it's just us praising my beauty. Care to join?" Stefen asked and chuckled. "You'll never get tired of this, do you?" Harry smiled and sighed.

Harry looked at Rya. She is staring at him. She lost it in her thoughts. Say nothing, but keep looking at him with a sharp face. Harry got really scared by that face.

"Mm, did I do anything wrong?" he asked with a pitiful face.

Stefen can't hold back his laugh. Rya keeps staring at both of them though. Harry got really confused. But he finds it funny too.

"So…mm, are you two staying home tomorrow?" Harry asked to change the atmosphere nervously.

"Yeah, since it's a weekend. I guess it's better to stay at home. We really don't spend much time there." Stefen said and looked at Rya. She nodded like she is also agreeing with that.

"So, what's your plan? Are you going home or are you going to spend your time in your apartment?" Stefen asked.

"Well, I'll spend my time in the apartment. It's better to stay there than going home." Harry replied.

"Why don't you like going home?" Rya asked curiously.

"It's more like, it's not my home. I never saw my parents. When I was little, around a 5-year-old, I was living with my uncle. But a young boy just like my age came to me one day and asked me to go with him. I refused, so my uncle. But the next morning my uncle and family disappeared. That boy and his family came again and forced me to go with him and after that his family adopted me." Harry said, lowering his head.

"They are kind to raise you, aren't they?" Stefen asked.

"Yeah, more like enslaved than raise. They gave me shelter in a Darkest room and asked me to do all the work. Even as a little kid I was forced to do every work. It's just a horrible life. But when I got admission here, I was so happy. After all, I can come here and study and build a good life. Maybe I wish I could find a real family." Harry said and smiled at them.

They never knew Harry had lived a life like this. They want to comfort him. But they don't know how to. They just smiled at him and spoke

"Yeah, now you have found one. We are your family now. Ok?"

"Yeah, now I have you. Harry smiled with tears. "Ok, I've got an idea! Don't spend your time in your apartment tomorrow. Come to our home. Let's hang in there." Rya said.

"Yeah, I think it's a great idea. What did you say?" Stefen asked.

"I'm honored." Harry said with a smile and teary eyes.

I'm grateful to say I've you! He said in his mind and held back his tears. But the pain in his heart never stops.

One of Us

[Morning, Rya's and Stefen's mansion]

"Good morning, little princess. Your Harry will be here in any minute. Aren't you excited?" Stefen laughed.

"Excuse me, my Harry? When did he become mine?" Rya sulked.

"Well, just assume he is mine!" Stefen said.

"Mine or yours, what is it?" Rya teased.

"Mine. No, I mean yours" Stefen confused.

"Yeah, yours….?" Rya laughed at Stefen dramatically.

"Well, you know what I mean. Don't make me confused." Stefen said and laughed.

"Then tell it clearly." Rya laughed

"Harry is Rya's" Stefen said loudly.

"Oh Stefen, we can hear you. Don't be so loud. You're making as deaf." Rya said.

"Oh yeah…? Then tell me what I said!" He said and started to tease her. He keeps saying that loudly and loudly. She asked him to stop but he kept teasing her.

"Fine, I'll say. If I say, will you please stop this nonsense?" she sighed.

"Well, I'll try." Stefen laughed.

"Harry is Rya's! Ok?" she aggressively asked.

"What?" Harry suddenly asked. He was standing beside Rya.

She feels so embarrassed like she couldn't look at him. She stared at Stefen like she wanted to throw anything at him. Stefen keeps laughing while slapping Harry. He couldn't stop his laugh when looking at Rya's embarrassed face. Harry just stands there like he has no idea what's going

Stefen showed Harry their home. Rya keeps following them remembering all the good times she had there. They showed their childhood photos with their parents too.

Harry looks at them like there's something bothering him.

"So how is our home? Is it beautiful like me?" Stefen asked and chuckled.

"Well, it's so beautiful!" Harry said and sighed.

"Well, what's so important to being beautiful? It's so empty now; it's not felt like home anymore." Rya said desperately.

"I don't think home is a place to call where you just born and grown." Harry said while looking at Rya's childhood photo.

"Then, what do you think to call home?" Rya asked curiously. Stefen is also looking at Harry with the same curiosity as Rya.

"Huh, how do I say? Home is someone or somewhere where you learn to love, live, dream and where your memories lie. It'll never be empty. Even if the person is not with you or you are not in the same place anymore it'll not change, it'll be not empty. So, we can always cherish those memories, and always feel home by just closing our eyes; we can live in those memories. It's enough to live an eternity." Harry said with his eyes closed, tears floating on his cheeks and a little smile on his lips and holding the same photo of Rya.

Rya and Stefen were so stunned to speak. They felt heavy in their hearts. They just keep walking through the house thinking about what Harry said. They were smiling with their beautiful memories.

[Upstairs]

"Well, this is the last room to show you. It's my uncle's official room." Stefen said while looking at Rya.

"We plan to set this room today. Since you're here you have to help. Do you have any objections?" Stefen added.

"No. I would like to help." Harry replied with a smile.

"Then come on. What are we waiting for?" Rya said while opening the door.

There're so many books in a big bookshelf there. Some books were kept on the table.

"So, what are we going to do here?" Harry asked.

"Well, we have to set the shelf, table and all the books. My father didn't allow anyone to do it. Before he died, he asked no one to come to this room. Only me and Stefen are allowed. So that's why not any servants have been here since then." Rya said with a deep breath.

"So, am I allowed?" Harry asked, looking at Rya.

"You are!" She doesn't know how to answer that.

She asked herself that question. Who is he to them? She doesn't have an answer but deep down her heart was telling her he is not a stranger, not anybody but someone she cherishes or maybe someone she missed.

"You're one of us now, brother. You're family." Stefen just fills the silence. They all look at each other. It feels so good to all of them. They just feel like there's a missing part that is filling in.

Stefen feels strange like on the other side of the window someone is watching them. It's a feeling he used to know. Ever since they got back to this town, from the first day of university, he could feel that someone was watching them. 'Who is that? Is that the same boy I met at the university? Why did he follow us? He always kept asking those questions himself. Yet he misses even it's a feeling when it's not around.

Stefen looks at Rya. She is also looking over the window. He knows she also got the feeling. What surprised him was that Harry is also looking out the window with his pitiful eyes.

Stefen and Harry were arranging the shelf and books. Rya was clearing the books on the table. She got a strange book. It's a mirror covered on the front and red velvet cover on the backside. There's a title on there too; 'THE CHILD OF UNIVERSE'. She looked at that book. She can see her face in the mirror just below the title. She kind of liked that book, so she asked Stefen and Harry to take a look.

"Wow, it looks so beautiful. Is this a story book? It looks like royalty." Stefen shared his affection for that book.

"I liked this too" Harry joined them.

"Come on open up. Let's see what it is about." Stefen can't control his curiosity.

Rya opened that book. But unfortunately, the language used in it is out of their knowledge. She keeps turning the page. They found something interesting in it. The birth marks they have, that's in the book.

For Rya; a triangle on the right-hand palm and a sun on the right-hand wrist.

For Stefen; a balance or karma sign on the right-hand wrist.

For Harry; a moon on the right-hand wrist.

"Maybe it's a book explaining our birthmarks. I always wondered about this." Stefen said and looked at his mark.

"But this language, do you ever see this?" Rya asked with a disappointed face.

"No, but it must be something like that. Maybe it's connected to our families. Look, it has Harry's birthmark too." Stefen grabbed that book and turned that page to show to them.

"Maybe Harry is also a royalty. Maybe he is also connected with our family. Now it all makes sense, is that why we all feel connected. Don't you think so?" Rya excitedly said. She looks at Harry.

Harry just standing there says anything. He just keeps looking at them without any words.

"Why are you so silent? Say something." Rya concernedly said to Harry.

"I don't know anything." Harry said with his head.

"Are you alright brother? What happened?" Stefen asked worriedly.

"Yeah, I'm alright. I just feel uneasy…. I don't know…. I'm sorry." Harry said with a low voice.

"It's ok, come on, let's continue what we did. Then let's go outside." Stefen suggested.

"Yeah, that's a better idea. I'll keep this book here for now." She placed that book on the upper shelf and spoke.

"Brother, do you want to rest, take it. It's alright we're about to finish it. You helped enough!" Stefen said concernedly.

"No, I'm good to go. It'll finish soon anyway. I've done far more than this, so don't worry. Let's continue." Harry said and smiled.

They knew there was something bothering him. They thought maybe it's his childhood memories. They knew it's not easy for him. They finished their work; Rya saw a door just behind the shelf. It's so mysterious. That door doesn't have any lock to open. It's plain. Rya was so shocked. She called Stefen and Harry to show them the door.

"Look at this door!" Rya screamed. "What door?" Stefen panicky asked. Harry tagged along too.

"This! Look at this door. It's so mysterious…. How do we open this?" Rya asked surprisingly.

"What's so special about this? It looks so normal. We can open this door like……" Stefen said this and stood there for a second quietly. "Oh my god it has no lock…." he screamed excitedly.

"Oh my god look at this Rya it has no lock, how do we open this?" Stefen couldn't control his excitement.

"Yeah, no wonder dad never let anyone come here. He must be hiding or protecting something. What is in there? How do we open it?" Rya asked again. They continued their same conversation for a long time.

"Is that the same thing you two asked again and again? You guys really never change." Harry said. He stood there watching their excitement all along.

"Huh, never change?" Stefen asked surprisingly.

"Ooh, why did I just say that? Never mind. Could you please stop it already? Just ask anyone about this door. Maybe you can ask your uncle, or anyone." Harry suggests.

"That's right. Let's call uncle. He might know something." Rya said.

Stefen called him immediately.

[Through call]

"Hello uncle, do you know about any mysterious door in the official room?" Stefen asked eagerly.

"Yeah, I might know something." uncle replied.

"So, you know how to open it?" Rya asked, hoping for a solution.

"All I know is that, that door is only open by you." Uncle said.

"By me, what do you mean?" She was stunned.

"You're the only one who can open that door. That's what your father said to me. I'm sorry. I can't give you more answers." uncle gives his answer to her. They hang up the call.

"Come on, let's find it later. We're getting so serious. We can find it eventually." Stefen said to make her ok.

"Yeah, that's right. Come on, give your guest some food, I'm hungry." Harry plays along with Stefen.

"Hey, you are not a guest anymore. I told you already you're our family now." Stefen said to Harry, but the situation became more awkward.

They talked for a long time, had fun. It's a lovely day for them. That long day feels like a short day to them.

"I have to go back. It's already late." Harry said and moved towards the door.

"Brother, can you stay here with us? We have so many spare rooms." Stefen said to Harry. Harry paused and turned to him, surprised. Rya is also surprised by the sudden question, even though it's the same thing she hopes for too.

"It's just since you came to our life, Rya seems so happy. Not only Rya, so am I. I just feel like I found my lost brother. We can share our holiday like this together. Come on, please. It's not felt like an empty home anymore." Stefen said awkwardly.

Rya laughed suddenly. "You look like a crying cute little child asking their parents not to leave." She teased Stefen. Harry joined with Rya too. He also laughed.

"Come on Harry, don't leave your child. Stay with him." Rya said to tease Stefen.

"Don't act foolish. You also want him to stay, don't you?" Stefen wants to tease Rya too. Soon after, they started to tease each other.

"Fine, fine…. I'll stay. But I've to take my things. I'll go get it. Ok?" Harry meddled again in their quarrel.

"I'll lend you, my things. You can take yours tomorrow, so you don't have to drive at night. What do you think?" Stefen asked.

"Fine then let me stay with you, your majesties." Harry asked and laughed. "Pleasure is ours!" they replied together to him. The cold breezes touch the longing.

Filling the Missing Parts

[At midnight]

There was thundering, lightning and strong wind. The sky becomes even more than Dark.

Suddenly Rya startled from her sleep. She screamed. In her scream it felt like the whole world was shaking.

Stefen and Harry ran into her.

"What happened?" Harry asked worriedly.

"Are you alright? Is it a nightmare?" Stefen was so worried too.

"Something bad is happening.... It hurts, it hurts me...." She screamed again.

"Where does it hurt? Could you get up? Let me take you to a doctor." Stefen said and held her hand.

She was shivering. It is more like she is afraid. She's sweating badly.

"I don't want to go anywhere. Here, stay here with me.... Don't go... don't leave me...." she cried holding her chest. That's when they know she has been hurting her heart.

They both hold her, even though she is in the arms of them; she cried about the fear of losing it. But in the comfort and the love of them she fell asleep holding them tightly.

[Morning]

"Young master, there is a guest waiting outside." Maid said to Stefen.

"Guest, this morning, who is it?" Stefen asked.

"He said he is Harry's brother." Maid answered quickly.

"Harry's brother? Let him in. I'll bring Harry." Stefen said confusedly.

"Yes, as you wish." She said and left.

The maid goes downstairs to let him in. Stefen knocks Harry's door to tell he has a visitor to go down, but there's no answer. So, he goes downstairs to greet the guest for Harry.

Stefen saw someone on the entrance door entering their home.

He is a young man, around 22 years old. He has Dark black hair and Dark black eyes. He looks like a Dark night.

When Stefen saw him, Stefen felt so angry and mad somehow.

"Hey I'm Dani, you must be Stefen. You didn't change at all." That young man comes forward to Stefen.

When Stefen heard his name, he remembers when Harry said about his uncle and his son. Dani it's him, the uncle's son who makes Harry's life miserable. Stefen wants to throw him out at an instance, but for the sake and respect to Harry he just stands nicely.

But still he feels so much anger towards him, and he wondered why.

"Why do you keep him around you every time? Huh, what is he good for? He is such a dog." Dani said arrogantly to Stefen and laughed at his face.

Stefen is covered in anger; in his anger even, the wind becomes hot.

"Don't say anything about him carelessly. Who are you to call him dog? How dare you talk aggressively about my brother?" Stefen said so angrily.

Dani came forward and stood in front of Stefen face to face and said; "oh Stefen, you're still that caring loving idiot." And starts to laugh aggressively and look Stefen angrily and arrogantly said again; "and see where it puts you." he continued.

Stefen feels like he is standing in front of a demon. In his eyes there is both fear and anger. Fear of losing something and anger for losing everything. Suddenly someone grabbed Stefen's shoulder. He felt at ease. He turned and looked. It's Harry.

Harry pulled Stefen and stood in front of him face to face with Dani.

"What are you doing here?" Harry asked angrily.

"I'm here to check you. I want to know how you are doing. You know I was sure you must find someone to be their dog. How pathetic are you?" Dani said arrogantly to Harry to make him feel uneasy.

"It's none of your business. You and I, we have no relation to each other." Harry said to Dani angrily.

"Oh, don't say that. I'm not done with you. 'I'll bring you down to the ground and haunt you at the very last.' Dani looked angrily at Harry. "I'll make you wish 'if you were never born'. So don't say we have nothing to do with each other; this little happiness you have now, I'll make that most grief again and again and again." He started to laugh aggressively again. And he looked at Stefen and said; "It goes for you too Stefen. I'll make your all-little happiness into the most grief." Dani said and smirked.

Harry brought him close to Dani and said; "If you touch anyone one of my loved ones, you'll be the one who wishes you were never born." In Harry's eyes he saw the anger and rage, and for a moment Dani felt fear.

"You still dare to threaten me, how dare you?" Dani angrily said to Harry. Harry keeps staring into his eyes with rage and anger.

On the upstairs, Rya feels like something bad is going on in there. At the very moment Dani came into that house, she felt uneasy. She wanted to get up from her bed, but she couldn't. She felt like she had been enchanted or something. But with the anger and fear of something; she broke that enchantment and ran into the stairs.

From the up she saw a boy standing in the main hall, he also looked at her.

When she saw him, she felt the most rage and anger. Every step she took in the stairs the ground was shaking. The wind became aggressive. She keeps stare at him with anger, in her rage she loses her control.

Suddenly Harry comes forward and stands in front of Dani. And he called "Rya" in his worried voice. When she saw Harry and heard him calling her name, she felt conscious.

"Get out now." Harry said to Dani.

"Well, I'm leaving now. But don't think it's over. It's getting started, we all see each other again and again from now on. The game starts now." Dani said and looked at everyone with a smirk and anger and started to walk outside.

He paused at the entrance and turned into Rya and said; "Let's meet again soon Rya." He took another step and Stefen closed the door in his face.

They all were in anger and rage but didn't ask anything to each other; because they knew it's more than Harry's evil brother and it's just the beginning of something.

[Outside]

Dani walked outside, and paused and said; "I knew you'd be here, the guardian dog." And he turned. The same boy Stefen met at the university on the first day is standing behind Dani.

"You still dared to come near them after all, what did you do to them? Do you really think they forgive you?" Dani mockingly asked him. He stares at Dani angrily.

"Don't be so brave. Don't forget you're still in my control. Not only you, if I want, I can easily take all of their life. So don't you dare to give me that look. Now come with me, I want to find that bastard who interrupts my plan every time, that unknown spirit." He said angrily and vanished in the wind.

That boy looked at the door, his eyes became teary. He said "I'll protect you this time." He closed his eyes and vanished in the wind, but the tears dropped in there.

[Rya's room]

"Hey, are you alright?" Harry knocked on Rya's door and asked. She was sitting on her bed trying to figure out what's going on. When she heard Harry ask, she nodded and tapped slightly next to her for Harry to sit there.

"Everything seems different somehow, like it's not what we used to live before. Since we came into this town everything started to change. Don't you think so?" Rya asked Harry with her tired eyes.

"My life started to change a long time ago. But I can say it's getting better ever since you came into my life. I'm sorry for what happened today." Harry said to Rya and held her hand.

"It's not your fault, then why are you apologizing? It has nothing to do with you. For some reason, I hate him so much. I don't know why but I never felt anything like this before. It's…. I don't know." She sighed.

"What about me, do you hate me too? Do you feel anything about me?" Harry asked Rya and looked at her. She is too stunned. She looked at him. Their eyes met.

He asked again; "Tell me." He keeps looking in her eyes. She doesn't know what to say. For her, from the very first moment they met she started to fall in love with him or it started before that. She used to dream of him, yet didn't know him. Since she started to dream about him as a child, she has liked him. That man is now asking her; does she hate him; does she have felt anything for him. But despite her feelings she is confused about everything going around her.

"Come in brother. You still haven't changed." Harry laughed and spoke. Stefen is behind the door hearing their conversation.

"How did you find me? I was standing there being quiet." Stefen asked curiously.

"Yeah, you stand there quietly, but you were laughing out loud." Rya said and smiled.

"Oh, am I?" Stefen asked dumbly. "Oh, but what did you mean by still haven't changed?" I never did this earlier, right?" Stefen asked Harry.

"Yeah, that's right. It just comes from nowhere, never mind." Harry said doubtfully and shook his head.

"Well, why are you peeking? You can just come and join us." Rya said to Stefen and pinched his hand.

"I'm not peeking. You never understand this, you know my little princess, my beautiful sister and my best friend my brother....... it's so wonderful....... You'll never get it." Stefen sighed with a smile.

"Hey, what are you implying? We were just having a normal conversation. Come on Harry, why are you silent? Say something." Rya said arguably and tried to cover her shyness.

"Am I your best friend? I'm so happy." Harry said and sniffled. At that moment Stefen sniffled too. They just hug each other.

"Well, you know, maybe you just tried to work out. You two make a perfect couple." Rya said and laughed. Suddenly they just push each other.

"No, no. Harry is yours. I have someone out there somewhere. I just have to find them. Well one day I'll meet them and just start to like them. Who knows, maybe I'll start liking them before I actually see them." Stefen said with a big smile. Rya looked at Harry; she just felt something in her heart. He also looked at her.

"Then tell me, what type of person do you want?" Harry asked Stefen.

"I want someone who can love me at my worst. Who can love and accept my sister like me and if they look anything like Rya, then it's perfect. I just want someone like that." Stefen said and took a deep breath.

"I hope you get someone like that as soon as possible." Rya said so happily. They all smiled and tried to forget all the worries they had until now, not knowing what awaits them. Stefen just felt a familiar breeze touch his heart.

[Three days after at university]

Stefen and Harry were sitting in their classroom. Rya came to call them and waited for them at the door. Harry suddenly jumps from his seat and grabs his bag. Stefen is still in a sleepy mood, so he sits there and watches both Rya and Harry just scrolling his eyes. Harry takes Stefen's bag and drags him from his seat.

"What took you so long? I was about to go." Rya said so disappointedly.

"Ask your brother; he is sleeping all day today." Harry said and looked at Stefen. He's still half asleep. "Come on, let's drink something." Rya said while shaking Stefen.

They were enjoying sitting on a bench in the university ground; in the cold breezes and watching the beautiful atmosphere.

"You know uncle called me today? He's so mad that we sent off all the maids. Somehow, I told him to relax; we're going to be okay. He asked me the reason; I told him it's maybe the right thing to do. Who knows what's coming to us." Stefen said.

They both looked at him and said nothing. But Stefen is still half asleep. He put his head on Rya's shoulder and had a nice nap.

"Hey, you're here!" A boy came to Rya and asked very happily.

"Oh hey, it's you. How're you?" Rya asked him.

"Fine, I was looking for you actually. How're you doing?" He asked with a smile.

Rya looked at Harry, she can see him burning with a jealousy flame.

"Yeah, I'm better. This is my brother; Stefen." She said while looking at her Stefen who is still sleeping on her shoulder.

"And this is Harry. He is…. Um…" She looked at him, "He is family." She continued.

"This is Jay. He is from my department. We met sometimes. We choose the same major." She said and looked at Harry like trying to calm him down.

"Hey." Harry just nodded and spoke.

"We can see at our classes." She smiled and spoke. She wants him to go because she can see Harry staring into his soul jealousy.

"Yeah…? Sure." He looked at Harry and Rya and just walked away.

There was silence around them for a moment. On the other side, Stefen chooses to sleep and never mind anything.

Suddenly a strong sharp wind came. The sky started to become Dark. The atmosphere became dull from pleasant. Rya held Harry's hand and looked at the sky with fearful and worried eyes. But in her eyes, there is also anger and vengeance. Harry holds Rya's hand tightly to remind her, he is with her. Stefen can also feel something off. He sat there and said nothing. They together were finding comfort in each other.

"Hey, you remember me? Huh, you must probably miss me." Suddenly someone said behind them. They turn and look at them. It's Dani. He is still arrogant and has a creepy smile on his face. But they notice he is not alone this time. There is a guy with him. He looks so familiar. Rya keeps staring at him.

"You're the same guy that day I met, on the first day of university?" Stefen jumped from his seat and asked.

"I don't know what you are talking about." That guy said,

Stefen felt confused but strange too, because he knew it was him but why did he deny? What's the feeling he has always had?

"No, I'm sure, it's you." Stefen argued. Dani looked at both of them and smirked.

"Well, this is my friend Sam. Huh guess like you already know him." he said arrogantly and sarcastically.

Rya kept looking at him; her eyes filled tears. She felt so heavy in her heart. She knows this familiar feeling. Harry stood there, watching everything. He looked at Sam and said nothing. He looked very angry. He asked Dani "What the hell are you doing here?"

"What a question? You already forget what I told you before? We're going to meet every now and then. Today I want you to meet my friend. He feels so delighted to meet all of you. Isn't it Sam?" Dani said so arrogantly.

They can't stand his arrogance. They feel so angry.

"It's nice to meet you Sam." Rya said with a shivering voice. She wants to talk to him more but she is afraid and confused about what's going around her and everything feels strange.

Stefen feels so bad for Sam but he is angry with him too, because he said he didn't know him. Stefen was dying to meet him again.

"Well, I have another surprise for you Harry, look at there." Dani said and turned his face over there.

There's a girl walking to them with an arrogant face. She looks the same age as Rya. She comes and holds Harry's hand. Rya looked at Harry brokenly.

"Hey, I'm Kate, Harry's fiancée. You must be his new friends. Huh......Nice to meet you!" she said and smirked at Rya's face.

She is still calculating what's going around her.

Harry pulls his hand from her and steps back a little.

"What the hell are you doing here?" Harry asked so angrily.

"Well, I missed you. What's more? I heard you were hanging with another girl here. Huh.... She must be the one who tried to steal you?" she looked at Rya and looked at her angrily.

"Mind your words! I don't care if you were related to Harry, but if you say another word like that about my sister, you'll know who I am." Stefen said so angrily.

"Oh, is that so? You must be the stupid brother who taught her little sister to steal another one's boyfriend?" she said to Stefen arrogantly.

"Shut up. Who the hell is your boyfriend? How dare you talk to them like this in front of me? Who the hell are you? Stay away from my life or you'll regret. And also, I'm not your boyfriend neither your fiancée. Do you get it?" Harry said to Kate and hold Rya's hand.

"Let's go." Harry looked at Stefen and spoke. Stefen nodded.

Dani was watching all the drama going around there and enjoying the miseries of them with a smirk. Sam stood there hopelessly to do anything. They looked at Sam while going.

Rya walked to him and said, "Can we see often, I don't know why but it feels like I know you somehow. Really, I don't know what's going around me, but I hope we can get along.

" She asked with her teary eyes. Her voice was shaking. Stefen also walked to them and looked at him with the same eyes as Rya. He can read the exact same things as Rya said from Stefen's eyes too.

Sam smiled at her with tears flowing on his cheeks and with a soft smile

"Yes…. We can." he looked at Harry. Harry was smiling at him with his teary eyes like he was saying; it's alright, you deserve it, you've done enough. Sam felt like he wanted to cry on his knees to them, he just felt there's something that was alive in him again.

[At their home]

Stefen was sitting on the couch. He was lost in thoughts and looking out of nowhere.

"Hey, what are you looking at?" Harry asks Stefen and sits next to him. He looked at Harry and sighed.

"I was thinking about that guy, you know the one with Dani today." Stefen said to Harry and looked nowhere again.

"You mean Sam? What's wrong?" Harry asked curiously.

"You know, I'm sure it's him that I met that day, but why did he lie to me? In fact, I was really glad to meet him again. But he just said he didn't know me……huh I just feel so angry at him." Stefen said and sulked.

"Maybe he has his reasons. Why do you care so much about him? Why've you so bothered about it?" Harry asked and looked at Stefen like he was waiting to hear something from his heart.

"I don't know…… I just felt I knew him actually … .it just you know…." Stefen really doesn't know what's with him.

"Does it feel like when you see Dani?" Harry asked nervously.

"Oh no, obviously not... I know he is your brother, no offence…. but I really…. really……hate him. It's like when I saw him, I wanted to throw him into the sea. Oh god I really hate him. But Sam…." Stefen stopped suddenly.

"But Sam…..." Harry asked with a smile on his face.

"I just felt sorry for him for some reason. I don't know why but I want to be friends with him." Stefen said with a sad look on his face. Harry looked at him and was about to say something.

"But you know you'll be my best friend. That'll never change." Stefen holds Harry's hand.

Harry nodded. Their eyes were filled with tears and smiles on their faces.

"Wow, I should write some books about brotherhood, the world will be jealous." Rya came in and said to them,

"The world may not be jealous but you will." Stefen said and laughed.

Rya looked at him angrily. "What makes you feel angry because I hold Harry's hand? Are you jealous?" Stefen laughed so loudly.

Rya throws a pillow at him which she got in handy.

"Well, I'm going, but don't be jealous because Harry loves me more than you, right Harry? You love your best friend more than your girl, right?" Stefen stood there and looked at Harry.

"You are not just my best friend, you're my soul brother. And I love both of you; my girl and my brother." Harry said, squeezing his fingers trying not to cry. His eyes were filled with tears.

"See, he loves both. Hmm, not just you, he also likes me." Rya said suddenly loudly to Stefen without realizing what she was saying.

"What, come again?" Stefen laughed. She realizes what she did just there. She slaps Stefen to hide her blushing. Stefen laughed at her again.

Harry looked at them with his teary eyes and a smile on his face.

[Later Rya's room]

Harry knocked Rya's room. "May I come in?" Harry asked to Rya.

"Yes." She said while looking at him.

"You know earlier, at university Kate, it's not what you think. She is my uncle's daughter. She was babbling about the whole fiancée thing. I didn't like her. She said she wanted to marry me when I was about to leave their house, they're saying I owe them my life. But I don't like her. I never did. I just wanted you to know. Stefen knows about this already. I never imagined she would come like this and make a scene. I'm so sorry…. I really am. If it hurts you somehow, please forgive me…." Harry said so worriedly.

"First take a breath. It's ok. I never took that into my heart. It's fine. But I have to say I really hate your uncle's both children. She even mocked my brother. And Dani, I don't know, but I hate him so much. How could you live with them all these years? Ooh, I was so lucky to have my brother by my side and also our family. I can't imagine what you have gone through. The way they are insulting you, mocking you and speaking to you, I hate it. I really hate it." Rya said to Harry.

He was standing there staring at Rya curiously.

"First take a breath. And what were I saying and what are you talking about? I said sorry for what happened. I didn't like Kate. I only like you!" Harry said to Rya and looked at her.

"Yeah, I know what you're telling you only like…. You what?" She suddenly realizes what he said.

"I said I only like you." He holds her arms and looks straight into her eyes and speaks.

She looked at his eyes too. She can see sea waves in his eyes. Her heart aches.

The longing, the regret, the missing and love, her heart can't take any of that. Her eyes were flowing with tears. She felt like going to faint. There are so many images shadowed at them instantly. The pieces in their heart started to stab them hardily. Harry saw her panicking. He feels like his heart is weighting, he can't take that pain anymore. She pushes Harry away.

"I don't know.... what are you talking about?" She turned and said without looking at him.

"Ye...ah......" Harry said. His voice was breaking.

He felt the room. He turned and looked at her. She is still not looking at him. He lowered his head and walked away. The longing and regret and above all of the pain of love in his heart, he felt it's going to break both his heart and soul.

"What are you doing? I think you liked him." Stefen came out suddenly.

He looked at Rya. She was shaking.

"What happened?" Stefen is concerned.

"You don't like him, or you think he is just joking around. Look, he is serious about you. Why are you being like this?" Stefen hugged her and patted her head.

"I know. I like him but I'm afraid.... I'm afraid I'll hurt him again. I love him.... but I'm afraid.... She shattered.

She cried in his arms like her heart was breaking.

"What are you afraid of? What are you talking about, I don't understand. I mean you two are perfect for each other. What happened?" he held her tightly and asked in a low voice.

"I don't know, but... I'm afraid.... I'm afraid I'll hurt him to death......" she fainted in Stefen's arms suddenly.

The regret and sorrow and the feeling of guilt for everything weighted down her heart and soul.

Hold on to Each Other

[Few hours later, Rya's room]

Stefen is sitting next to Rya. Rya is still unconscious.

"I'm sorry…. I'm sorry……Nooo ……." She screamed.

"Hey, are you alright? It's ok…. I got you. It's ok." Stefen holds her tight.

She was shaking. "Harry…. I'm sorry…. I…." she startled and jumped from her bed.

"Harry, where is he?" Rya asked Stefen.

"He is not in his room, but I'm sure he is around. Why don't you just have a little more rest. By the time you wake up I'll find him and bring him in to you. I promise. Please lie down a little bit…." Stefen said and patted her head concernedly.

"I hurt him again, I lost him again. It's my fault, every time. I always hurt him. I don't deserve him……." she cried and sobbed. Her heart aches. She cried and lay down there. She felt like her spirit left her body. She felt no strength.

Stefen got up and came out from her room after she fell asleep. He went to Harry's room. He is not there. He tried on his number, but no answer. He got worried. He looked for him everywhere in the house. On the way he came from outside to Ryan's room after looking for Harry, he suddenly saw Harry standing in front of his room.

"Where did you come from? I looked for you everywhere and even called you. But you didn't answer." Stefen asked Harry and curiously looked at him. But he felt at ease because Harry was right there with them.

"I was in the garden." Harry said in a low voice.

"Garden, but I did look there, but didn't see you. And how did you even come here? I didn't see you pass by?" Stefen asked curiously.

"I didn't see you either." Harry replied to Stefen without looking at him. Stefen feels bad for Harry, he knows he is going through a breakdown and he keeps asking questions.

"Rya, she fainted a little while ago…." Stefen said to Harry.

"Is she alright?" Harry asked panicky.

"Yeah, she is sleeping now. Guess like she is too tired. Hey brother, she was crying for you all this time. She is worried like she might hurt you again. She kept saying that…. She said she loves you. To be honest I never saw her like this broken. I don't know what got into her, but since we came here everything has changed. Even for me, I don't understand anymore what's going on around us. I know it's the same for you too. But I strongly believe it's something like destiny that we all met each other. Maybe that's why we all got this bond." Stefen said to Harry and sighed.

"You know what, I strongly believe you'll be the one who protects her, and in fact you'll be the only one who can protect her. I don't know if it sounds weird; but will you give me a promise that you'll always be with her and protect her and make her happy. She needs you brother. I know her, she really likes you." Stefen continued.

His eyes filled with tears. Stefen's heart felt a little comfort after saying all this. He looked at Harry like he was waiting for a reaction.

"You talk too much brother. But I promise, even if I have to give-up everything, I'll protect her." Harry said and wiped his tears and smiled through the pain. Stefen smiled at him back.

Harry doesn't know what his heart felt that moment when Stefen said all of this. He asked himself 'can he protect her? Can he make her happy? He can be with her forever?'

They walked into Rya's room. When they entered her room, she slowly opened her eyes. Her eyes were tired with all this crying. She looked at Harry. They both didn't know what to say to each other. They kept quiet.

"I brought you your Harry as I promised. You two talk and make up with each other. I've got something to take care of." Stefen said and left that room. The room felt totally quiet for a moment. Harry just sat there beside her.

"Are you feeling better now?" Harry asked concernedly.

"Yeah, better now." She said and looked at his face.

"I'm sorry if I let you down. Actually I……." she sniffled.

"It's okay Rya; you don't have to worry about me. Whatever happens I'll be besides you like this and always with you. Even if you hate me, I'll do whatever it does take to protect you. I promise." He held her hands and spoke.

"I know." She holds his hand back tightly. That's enough for them to understand that in this world they are only for each other.

"You know where Stefen's went?" She asked him to sit-up. She was careful not to let go of his hand.

"As I know him, he must be behind that door?" Harry laughed and looked at the door.

"How do you find me every time? I was being careful not to laugh." Stefen said and sulked.

"Here he is." Harry laughed.

"Really guys, I was really impressed. To be honest I never saw any bond like this. Are you sure you two met recently?" Rya asked with a little jealousy.

"Who knows?" Harry said and smiled.

"Look who's talking, holding hands huh……." Stefen said dramatically to mock her. She holds his hand even tighter.

"Yes I'm." she raised their hands and said proudly.

They laughed all together. They're ready to face whatever is coming. They know in their heart they will always have each other.

[On the other side, twilight time]

Sam is sitting on top of a high building. He can view their home from afar. He looked there and his eyes filled with tears and lost in thoughts.

"I know you'll be here." Suddenly Dani came and spoke.

"What do you want?" Sam asked him not to look at him and in a rough voice.

"Did you do what I just asked? Did you find him? He must be somewhere here definitely. Go find him." Dani said angrily.

"I can't find him, why don't you try yourself? You claim you're strongest every time, isn't it? Then why don't you catch him yourself?" Sam asked sarcastically.

"Don't mock me. You think I haven't tried. All these hundreds of years I was searching for that stupid unknown spirit. Every time I'm about to win, he just keeps killing me. He is just playing a damn hide and seek. But when I get him, he'll regret playing with me." Dani said very angrily.

Sam smirks at him sarcastically. "What? I can find him, before that, you know what I'm going to do. I'm going to kill them, your dears' ones, once again. You think I can't do that?" Dani asked arrogantly.

"You wouldn't. You want to know where the Trio World is. That's the only reason you didn't even try to kill them. You want them to have their memories back, and you want to know what happened to the Trio World. Is this correct? But you have other reasons too. Tell me the truth Dani; you scare him, don't you? The one keeps disturbing your plans. You know they are under their protection. You're scared to mess with him, don't you? Every time you come this close to get what you want, he just keeps making you. What if he is the one who finds them first? What if he helps them against you? Can you imagine how miserable it will be?" Sam asked arrogantly.

"Do what I told you; don't forget you're still in my control. Even if you get your consciousness back, it doesn't mean you broke the chain. And don't be so arrogant. You think they will forgive you for what happened that day? For what do you all these years helping me? I'll never let any of you live peacefully. And that unknown spirit, he is my headache. I'll find him myself soon and he's going to regret what he is doing to me." Dani said angrily and vanished in the wind.

"You alright guys? This time I will protect you no matter what. It's my entire fault for the beginning. I'm sorry." Sam said and kept looking at that house from faraway.

[Next day]

Rya was waiting for Stefen and Harry on the outside of their university with her friend Jay. "Here they come." Rya pointed a little far. Stefen and Harry were walking to them.

"That's the guy I told you before." Harry whispered to Stefen.

"He is handsome." Stefen said to Harry. Harry glanced.

"But you're much more handsome than his brother. Don't take it as a competition. He is just a friend." Stefen said and patted him. They reached them.

"Hey, I'm Jay. We met each other the other day. She told me you're her brother. It's nice to meet you brother." Jay said and smiled. "Yeah, it's nice to meet you too. She told me about you too." Stefen replied.

He looked at Harry. Harry is in real anger. The way he calls Stefen; 'brother' he doesn't like that much.

"Actually, it's great to see my little sister make friends with everyone." Stefen said and glanced at Harry to make him jealous.

"No, not everyone. Actually, he told me an interesting story. So, we just became close." Rya said excitedly.

"Ooh what is it? Let me hear?" Stefen asked.

"Ooh actually it's some kind of belief in our family. You can call it a myth. That there are some powers that protect the world and us. Actually, the power of the universe is assorted; mainly by some people. I don't know about the whole details, but I remember when my grandmother told me this amazing story; that there is this girl with golden hair and golden eyes. Even her skin is gold. She is brighter than the sun. The peace, the light and the love we have and to each other now, is the sacrifice of her. Not only hers but also her companions. I had this big book about this entire story in my home. My mother said it is sacred." Jay said looked at Stefen and Harry.

Stefen was staring at Rya and Harry was just curiously looking at Jay.

"The girl you described is just like Rya, isn't she?" Stefen asked curiously.

"Isn't it? I'm not that into believing. But when I saw Rya; I just felt like I met the goddess in my grandmother's stories." Jay added.

"What's your family name?" Harry asked Jay.

"Ooh mine, it's 'shines', we know like that. What? Do you know my family?" Jay curiously asked.

"No, no I was just asking." Harry shakes his head. Being jealous, he just looks a lot in pain after Jay's story. Not only him but Stefen were lost in thoughts too.

"Actually, I waited here to invite you two to my birthday party. It's next week, I don't have that many friends. So, I hope you can make it." Jay said nervously and looked at Stefen and Harry.

He knows Harry was jealous and doesn't like him that much. Rya and Stefen also looked at Harry, they were afraid he will be mad. Stefen was about to say sorry to Jay.

"We'll come. Don't worry. We'll be there." Harry patted his shoulder.

Rya and Stefen looked at Harry surprised.

"So, where are you going?" Suddenly Dani appeared and asked.

He is with Sam. When Rya saw Sam, she smiled at him.

But Stefen just turned his head and stood there being mad. "So, you've now got friends to invite you to their little parties. That's interesting." Dani added sarcastically.

"It's none of your damn business." Harry said angrily.

"Ooh, don't be like that brother…we still have some business with each other." Dani said to Harry and turned into Jay and said; "Are you not going to invite us to your party?"

"Yeah sure, it's on next week. Please come." He nervously said.

"You come too." He looked at Sam and spoke.

"So, Jay isn't? Where are you from?" Dani asked suspiciously.

"My family has lived here for years now, basically I have no idea about ancient history. But since I was born, I have lived here. Why do you ask?" Jay asked him to look at him.

"No reason, I just want to know…." Before Dani done his talking Harry said to Jay

"You done right? You can leave now. We'll come to your party." When he said that, Rya and Stefen looked surprised.

Because they knew he was protecting Jay from Dani. Jay just nodded and left. He also feels uncomfortable around Dani.

"Wow, look someone now capable of protecting people around him, since he can't protect himself." Dani said angrily.

"I can protect myself and I will protect my loved ones. Stay away from them." Harry said in a warning tone, and his eyes were burned in rage.

Sam came forward and said hello to Harry. Harry just felt at ease and nodded at him. Sam smiled at Rya and Stefen too. Rya smiled at him back and waved her hands. The only thing she likes when Dani arrives is; he brings Sam with them. But Stefen, he just turned and face and sulked.

"How're you doing? It's nice to meet you again." She said happily.

"Yeah, for me too." he said and smiled.

He looked at Stefen, he was still mad. "Looks like someone is still mad at me?" He said to Rya and looked at Stefen.

"Believe me, he is such a sweetheart, he is just sulking." Rya said and smiled.

Stefen just glanced. "I know that. If he is mad, I deserve it." He said with a smile and tears in his eyes. Stefen looked at him.

He just felt that being mad at Sam is unreasonable. He just wants to say 'hey', but before that Dani said to Sam; "Enough with the chit chat. Let's go."

Rya looked at Sam unhappily. She doesn't want him to leave with Dani. He just patted her head and nodded his head. She doesn't know what happened, in her heart; it felt like a cold breeze touched her heart's wound. She wants to talk to him; she wants to pat him.

But before that she could say anything, he was just standing there beside Dani. She feels like she wants to drag him from his side and just wants him to stay beside her and be with her and him to take care of her. She wants him to be……her heart suddenly found something….

She wants him to be her 'Big brother'.

She mumbled and looked at him; "Big brother."

That moment everyone just stood there shockingly. There are pieces in their heart that have started to become painful. Sam looks so happy and painful at the same time. He wants to cry so loud, but he just lowers his head, his tears start to wet his feet.

Harry and Stefen looked so surprised. Stefen just stands there like 'what'.

Harry doesn't really know what he felt at that moment. He just keeps looking at both Sam and Rya. Dani suddenly laughed evilly.

"Well, well." He said and gave a deadly look to everyone. At that moment even the wind can guess it's about to start everything.

[Few days later]

Stefen was sitting on his couch. Harry comes in and squeezes there.

"What are you thinking about? You look distracted this whole week. What's the matter?" Harry asked Stefen worriedly.

"I don't know; it's just…. I don't actually know. It's just…. I don't know. It's nothing."

Stefen said and with a dull face.

"Oh, come on. Say it already, I hate when I see you like this… what's the matter? What's bothering you this much even if you don't want to share with us?" she worriedly asked from his behind and pressed his shoulders to comfort him.

"It's just that guy…. You know, it's been bothering me lately. Why is he hanging with Dani? Every time when I look at his face; it's like he bears something so much that…. he is dead inside. I feel sorry for him somehow and I just feel mad at him." Stefen lowered his head and head.

"You know, I also felt that too. He always has a sad look on his face. But I like him, I don't know why but… I just felt like he's one of us. I just felt that we slipped him from us…." Rya said sadly.

"You know…... I felt what you guys both felt. But can I ask you something Stefen; why are you mad at him? Are you mad at him like you're mad at Dani?" Harry asked right away.

"No, it's not. I was just mad at him because he told me he didn't know me. That's all. But for; Dani…... I hate him so much……it's like rage or something." Stefen said to correct them.

They just look at each other. "So do you like Sam?" Rya asked with a little smile.

"Oh, you are the one who called him big brother. How could you call that in front of me? I just feel like I'm dumped." Stefen sulked.

"I never dumped you. You are still my favorite and cute childish brother. It's just you know; I don't know I just felt like that somehow. It's like someone in my heart called out that loudly. I really felt that he is also my brother, I'm sorry." Rya holds Stefen's hand with a sorry face. He pinched her cheeks with giggles. She smiled with her eyes.

"Within two days it's Jay's birthday; we should go. Don't you think so?" Harry asked without a glance. "What changed your mind? I thought you didn't like him." Stefen asked curiously. Rya also looked at him to know the answer.

"First of all, I didn't hate him. It's just I don't have an impression on him. That's all." Harry said while getting up. "Well, what gave you the impression now?" Stefen continued with his curiosity.

"The story he told me. It gave me the impression." Harry raises his head and looks at them. They looked at him. He just walked to the door.

"You are going outside?" Rya asked.

"Yeah, I have something to do." Harry turned and spoke.

"Hey, you think Dani and Sam come to Jay's birthday?" Stefen asked Harry.

"I think he will." Harry said with an angry face and "I'm getting going then." He waved his hand and walked away.

"Are you excited about seeing Sam again?" Rya asked with a cunning smile.

"Shut up. I'm not. I'm just asking. You'll probably be the one who is excited about that." Stefen asked and sulked.

"Of course, I'm. Hey, next time you see him, go and do your makeup with him." she said and looked at him. He nodded.

[Days passed. Jay's birthday; at night, Jay's home]

Rya, Stefen and Harry parked their car on the porch and rang the bell of Jay's home. Jay opens the door.

"Happy birthday" [Unison voice]

He welcomed them into his house. Some of his friends and family members are there. He introduced his mother and grandmother to them. They were all excited to see them, not only because of the story; they were also the royal members which are respected. They were comfortable there.

Suddenly a bell ranged. He opened the door.

It's Dani. They stood there like he was expecting him. But he is alone.

Rya looked at Stefen with a depressed look. Stefen quickly noticed that Sam was coming from behind.

"Oh, here he is!" Stefen said excitedly.

Harry looked at Stefen with a cunning smile. Rya couldn't control her laugh. She never saw Stefen like this confused and excited before.

But there is also something worse. Kate came along with them too. Harry looked at Rya. She is trying to ignore that fact.

They all came together. Everyone around them were enjoying themselves and partying. But between them all there is this tension and rage.

Stefen looked at Sam. He was observing the surroundings. He is thinking about what happened the other day.

[Two days before]

{Kate's, Dani's and Sam's hideout; it's so Dark and horrific.}

"Why are you so eager to go to that boy's birthday party? What's the big deal?" Kate asked Dani.

"He knows about our world. He knows about Rya. I want to find out how he knows everything." Dani said.

"So, are you thinking that he is the unknown spirit?" Kate asked right away.

"No, but he said he has a sacred book of these stories in his house. I want to take it. That book must be written by that unknown spirit. If I can find that book there must be some clues." Dani looked at Sam and spoke. Sam just ignored him and sat where he was.

"Why do we have to wait till the birthday? We can go and take that book right away." Kate said arrogantly.

"You think I sit here like a fool? Until that boy is welcomed to his house we can't enter. That book he has is sacred. It contained magic, strong magic. We have to wait until that day and be careful." Dani said angrily.

He continued; "we're going together, and we have to find that book. It contains that unknown spirit's magic; we can find him through that book. So don't lose the chance. Find that book necessarily at any cost." He said something like an order. Sam just kept looking outside and sat there.

[..................]

Stefen keeps looking at him until he notices him. When Sam saw him Stefen nod his head while raising his chin. Stefen walked to him. They two looked at each other and stood there awkwardly.

"Hey I'm sorry for what I said that day. You know, when I said I didn't know you. I really am sorry." Sam said with a sorry face. Stefen just nodded.

"Are you still angry?" Sam asked nervously.

"No, I'm not. But why did you say that in the first place?" Stefen asked.

"I really don't know." Sam said and smiled. Stefen looked at him madly, but when he saw Sam smiling, he smiled along with him.

Rya was sitting near the window. It is quiet and calm. It's a little far from the party room. She looks at the sky while sitting there. She saw

Stefen and Sam together, she felt at ease. She looked for Harry but he was nowhere to be found. So, she walked around to find that place.

"Oh, here you are." Rya remembered that voice. It's Kate. She glanced at her and said nothing.

"Are you ignoring me? I'm warning you, stay away my boyfriend. He is mine. Don't think you will get him." Kate said with angrily and arrogantly. She continued saying like that.

Rya sat there and said nothing. She knew arguing with her was a waste of time.

"He owes this life to us. He will be with me or he has to die. I'll not let you two be together. Consider it a warning or you will regret it. You'll lose everything like always." Kate said angrily and she smirked at Rya.

"Who the hell are you to warn me? What did you say about him? He owes you nothing, neither he is your boyfriend or anything. So just shut up. And Harry is mine. Have you heard of 'Harry is Rya's'? Even the world can't separate us and you think you can? He is mine." Rya said with an angry face. Her eyes were glowing like a burning sun.

"She is right." Suddenly Harry came in and spoke. He can see Rya is in anger. He holds her hand. They look at each other.

He continued. "I only belong to her. So just stay away from my life." Harry said to Kate.

The look on his face made her terrified. Both Harry and Rya with burning eyes, she felt like a nightmare. She suddenly leaves that room quickly.

Harry holds Rya's arms. He looks at her eyes. It's so beautiful. "Rya, do you really mean what did you just say to her now?" Harry asked, whispering.

"I'm." she looked at his eyes. She felt like she was going to drown in that. She withdraws her eyes and suddenly turns her face. He can see she is blushing. He lifted her face.

He brings his face close to hers. They can hear their heartbeat to each other. It's so loud. He touches her lips with him. They closed their eyes. She kept her hand in his chest. He holds her face. A little breeze embraced them.

They look at each other. They smiled at each other. He held her hands and walked from that room to find their companions. They never realize that Dani was watching all of this and burning in rage and vengeance.

"Hey, where did you go?" Stefen asked to Rya and Harry.

"You have a new brother now. Why do you care?" Harry said and smiled at Stefen.

"Hey, he is not my brother." Stefen said immediately. He was worried that Harry would feel sad.

"Yeah, I'm his boyfriend." Sam said and laughed.

"Hey what are you saying?" Stefen was shocked. They all laughed together.

"You want to come with us?" Rya asked Sam.

"Maybe later…" He said to her, After the party they all said goodbyes and have no idea what's waiting for them from now on.

The jealous, anger and rage above all of that obsession with power were shadowing them.

Shadows v\s Light

[Rya's and Stefen's home]

In the early morning before the sunrise; they were all sleeping in their own rooms. Suddenly a strange sound and feeling came.

They all wake up startled. They went out.

It's getting Dark and Dark suddenly. When they noticed what's happening, they were frightened to death; there were creatures like shadows like a black smoke coming from the sky.

Rya screamed and holds Stefen's hand. He is stand there like a statue. He couldn't move. Harry stands there like that too. He holds both Stefen's and Rya's hand together. But he has no idea what he's going to do.

Suddenly these creatures started to attack them. They managed to dodge some of the first attacks. But the numbers of those creatures are increasing.

Harry stands there in front of them like a shield. When the attacks are getting immense, they can't do anything.

When a creature is about to come straight to them, Harry stands there in front of him. It came closer, he closed his eyes.

Suddenly a golden light hit that creature. That thing fell afar. He opens his eyes, and looks back. That light came from Rya. He looked at her shockingly.

She was shocked too. But she knows this is not the time for that. 'The one's she loves are about to die, so fight and protect them' there's an inner voice in her.

Stefen looked at her with frightened and shocked eyes.

There is golden light coming from Rya's hand. It's like lightning. She keeps attacking those creatures.

Suddenly Harry started to join her too. There is black light more like thunder coming from his hand.

Stefen stands there shocked. Those demon creatures started to increase more and more. Rya and Harry fight hard against them to protect each other with anger and agony.

Slowly Harry's left eye started to turn like a beast. Suddenly someone appeared in front of Stefen.

It's Sam. "What are you doing here?" Stefen asked Sam Shockingly.

"I'll tell you later." He said to Stefen while fighting against those demons with his golden magic blasts'. Stefen felt like his hands were hurting.

The mark on his wrist is getting bolder. He screamed because he couldn't take that pain. A demon creature ran towards him. Suddenly he leashed a silver strike.

They all fight along with each other.

And that opens the door into the past; where truly they are, and the answers to all the questions they had until now.

It brings them to the time where they belong.

The Trio World

A beautiful golden palace; everything is perfect and luxuries, a dignified royalty.

A courtier came into the main hall of that palace.

The king of Magic world Rex Golden Crown is sitting on his throne.

"Your Majesty, the Peace world's king, had a boy just now. He liked you to join with his happiness. He invited the respected royals of Magic World to join with his happiness." The courtier said humbly.

The king gets up from his throne and walks to the lady who holds a baby; "Here son, do you hear that; you just got another friend." He took that child to his arms and walked to the throne and sat there.

He said to the courtier; "Inform him it's my pleasure to join with his happiness." The courtier left that room. The king cuddled that baby.

A little while after a man and a lady came into that room. They are the parents of that child.

"Brother, did he cause any trouble to you?" that man asked. "Of course not, He's giving me company." He replied with a smile.

That man is the royal cousin and a dear brother to the king, Henry Golden Crown. He is given the name of 'Duke of the Magic world'.

That lady is the wife of that man and the mother, Rosella Golden Crown of his child named Samuele Golden Crown and called by Sam.

They were so loyal to the king. After the king they're the most powerful and respected persons in the Magic World.

His mother took him from the king's arms and said; "why don't you find a queen to give you company, then you'll have your own baby to accompany you all the time." She said to the king and smiled concernedly.

"She is the right brother; it's time to find your partner. You are the king of the magic world. This world needs a queen." He also shows his concern. The king smiled at them calmly.

"Do you hear about a prince born into the Peace World? The king invited us to join his happiness, let's go together. Ok. We have to bring him too. He is the prince of the Magic World." The king said, patting Sam's head peacefully.

They smiled and agreed with the king.

[The Peace World]

A big beautiful silver palace; it's so calm and peaceful.

There were so many royalties attending the function. The Magic world's king and his family enter.

They can see the Dark world's king; Axel Blackstone is standing beside the Peace world's king, Ade Silver star, carrying his child' Harryngton Blackstone, called by Harry who was born a few days ago.

The Magic world's king walks towards them carrying Sam. They greeted each other.

"Congratulations my dear friend." the Magic World's king said.

The Peace king smiled and said "Thank you my dear friend; I'm honored to have you all here. Meet my son Stefenswen Silvers Star. Call him Stefen". He introduced his child to the kings of both worlds.

They both blessed him. "How is it going there, mate? Is everything alright?" the king of the Magic world asked the king of the Dark world.

"Yeah, but I think someone from our royal house is helping the Dark shadows." He whispered to them.

"Why did you have that thought? Did you find something?" they asked worriedly.

"Yeah, I'm. I'm searching for more information. Until we get all the information let's keep it a secret between us." The Dark king said to the peace king and magic king. They all agreed to each other.

"So, when are you going to get married?" The Peace king asked the Magic king.

"When I find my right partner" He replied with a smile. "Hey, why don't you think about the princess of the Peace world, Princess Ava Silver Star, his little sister?" Dark king suggested while pointing to the peace king.

The Peace king looks so happy. The Dark king called for the duke of the Magic world and asked for his opinion. He seems so happy to hear that. Actually, he has that thought on his mind for a while already. They all ask the Magic king to think it through.

He is a generous and wise man so he said he wanted to ask the opinion of the peace princess before taking any decisions. They all agreed.

"Are you checking through what I asked?" the Dark king asked the Magic duke.

"Yes, but unfortunately there is not much evidence. But what I got was someone for sure." Magic duke answered to the Dark king.

"Oh, are you discussing what you told me before?" the Peace king wondered.

"Yes, we're. I ask his help through this." He answered.

"That's good." The Magic king said concerned.

They all have been friends since they were kids. Having a heavy burden on their shoulders they always rely on each other and always live harmoniously. They always share the happiness and worries with each other and find a solution for all of them together.

"What's the big conference here?" Dark king's brother Cyrus Blackstone appeared.

He is carrying his son in his hands; Daniel Blackstone called by Dani, who is little older than Harry by months.

The Dark king's brother is the duke of the Dark world, but he is always jealous of his brother having the throne and power.

"Nothing much, we're talking about the Magic king's marriage." The Dark king answered.

"Oh, that's an interesting subject. Have you found a bride?" He asked the Magic king.

"We're thinking about the marriage between my sister and him." Peace king happily said.

"Oh, your sister?" he asked.

"What's wrong with that?" the Magic king wondered.

"Nothing; who knows after marriage having the power and influence in both Magic and Peace you wouldn't dare to attack our Dark world and conquer The Universe?" he said without any concern. They all felt disgusted about what he said.

"You know what, you should try that. Maybe if you became the ruler of the universe with your power you should stop all those demon Dark shadows and go save the entire world." The Dark king added to save the atmosphere.

The Magic king felt at ease, because what he was afraid was that his dear friend would misunderstand like Dark duke said.

He just hugged him and said "let our kids do that job. After all is the prophecy. It's their destiny. I'm sure they'll find a way to stop them." They all looked at their kids.

"We still need a queen between them." Dark king smiled and said to the magic king. They all laughed.

Few days after the Peace king informed that the Princess is ready to be the bride of the Magic king. The Trio World is ready for a big festival; the Magic king's and Peace princess' marriage. They all went very well.

One year later the queen of the Magic world was conceived. Everyone was waiting for the day for the birth of that child. The destruction by the Dark shadows is getting immense.

And the day came, the Magic Queen gave birth to a beautiful little girl. They named her Ryana Golden Crown and called her Rya.

The Trio World praises her beauty 'Golden Princess.

But the Dark shadows were targeting her. Because they knew the prophecy that she'll be the one who can destroy them. So the king and others decided to keep her in the palace for two years and give her all the training. The calamity increased day by day.

[The Dark World]

The Dark king was cherishing his beloved son with his queen, Tiana Blackstone. Suddenly a number of Dark shadows appeared. He took his sword and fought against them very hard. Suddenly his brother, the duke of Dark world appeared there.

The Dark king asks him to protect his wife and son while is fighting. But that cruel brother; who is always obsessed with power and jealous of his own brother, takes the sword and stabs the Dark queen. She is a pure soul and always loved her family very much. Even though the duke was always mean to her she didn't hate him, but loved him as her own brother she wasn't aware of that attack. But as strong as she was, she managed to get up and go to her baby.

The Dark king was so shocked. He was always aware that he was obsessed with power, but he didn't think like this. In front of him his beloved wife is stabbed. He aggressively fights with all he gets.

But his brother went straight towards his son and wife and said; "Give-up my dear brother. Are you going to fight until someone gets to help, is that what you're thinking then you are wrong. No one is going to help you. I put a spell. Everyone is sleeping like their soul left. When they wake up, they hear their beloved king has died." He arrogantly said and laughed.

"You're the one who always helped them from inside, aren't you? How could you do that? Why are they helping them?" the Dark king asked shatteringly.

"Huh, helping them? I'm the king of the Dark shadows now. And now you know the answers for your questions. You know there are so many lives I've to take to get this stronger. Now you are no match to me. Soon after I'll conquer The Universe " He laughed again.

The king got angrier. He moves towards him. But that devil points his sword against the King's son and wife. The king paused.

"Spare them. You want my life right, take it. Leave them alone." He screamed.

"Well, I can't, he's a part of the prophecy and you know, I don't want something bothering me here. So, you all have to die." He arrogantly said.

The queen looks at his son's face. She didn't want him to die, even though she knew there was nothing much she could do to save their lives. She looked at the king. He can read her mind. He nodded.

There are so many Dark shadows that keep coming. He does a spell suddenly.

The king and queen, both are ready to sacrifice themselves to protect their son.

Their sacrificial magic succeeds. The whole palace awakens, the Dark shadows disappeared. And they managed to control Cyrus's evil power to protect the other children of prophecy by giving him a curse.

They kiss their son for the last time and become a magical shield to protect from the devils until he becomes strong.

The courtiers and maids all come quickly to the king's room when they hear the prince is crying nonstop. When they entered, they saw; the king and queen were already dead, the prince was safely on the bed and the duke was standing beside the prince. When he saw they were coming he acted innocently.

They worriedly asked what happened and he said; "It's his entire fault. He is cursed. He killed my dear brother and his wife. This child is cursed." He pointed towards the prince.

Everyone in that room looked at that little child shockingly, because they don't want to deny the fact that there is also another prophecy that, in the Dark world there'll be a child who is going to become the most powerful among the Dark shadows by killing his parents and becoming Dark shadow king.

They all believed it was Harry. And there starts his miserable life.

Every world was so shocked and shattered by the Dark king's death. The both king and the duke were shattered and broken by the news of their beloved friend.

But somehow, they knew it was not because of Harry and they decided to protect him at any cost. They said he is still a little kid so let him grow up and let's see what the future holds.

That decision made some bad thoughts on others, but they have to agree with the peace and magic worlds.

The next week the Dark' duke, who killed his own brother, was crowned and became the Dark king.

His shadow power started to weaken his body and he knew there were some doubts among them. He knew it's not easy to kill those children like in his state now, so decided to act not rashly and with other plans, because he knew that the both other worlds must take cautions from now on.

Destined Souls

Because of the threat, the Magic king let Rya grow only in the castle until she becomes the age of five. Because only from that age can she use magic from a level. Even though it's dangerous to let her outside as a child, he doesn't want his child to live in a cage.

For the Same reason Sam and Stefen also lived in the castle except they were only brought to see Rya and play and train with her. Under the direct care of the kings as kids they were trained to become the strongest and even Dani sometimes joins them.

As for Harry he lived as a curse in the eyes of others and lived lonely. He didn't even meet any of those after his parents died.

Rya becomes five. Even though there are dangers around them, the elders decided it's time to let them live.

Along with Rya, Stefen and Sam are going to the Dark palace for the first time. They always wanted to meet that unknown friend who they never saw but heard a lot from their parents.

(Dark world)

The beautiful world is like a starry night, but even in that beauty the dead is passing.

They reached the palace with their parents.

Rya started to walk around the palace alone. It's like she is looking for something. She walked through the corridor and at the edge she heard that someone was weeping. She peeked into that room. She saw a little boy in that Darkest room.

"Hey why are you crying?" Rya asked Harry. When he saw her, he hid behind the bed.

"Why are you hiding? Are you afraid of me?" she asked sadly.

When he saw he made her upset, he got up and said with his head "It's not that, I'm cursed. I don't want to put others in danger."

She moved forward to him and held his hand and asked "Do you want to become friends with me?" He looked at her. It's the first time someone asked him to be friends and also someone talking nicely.

He sniffled.

 "Are you sure? Do you really want to become friends with me?" Harry asked.

"Of course, come and meet my brothers. They also want to meet you." she said and dragged him from his room. She holds his hand and runs through the corridor.

He felt like in his lifetime it's the first time he saw the light in that Darkness.

Sam and Stefen are waiting for Rya to play, by the pool area. They saw she was coming from a little far. They ran into her.

"Where did you go?" Stefen asked concernedly.

"Look!" Rya shows Harry who is hiding behind her.

"This is Harry; he was sitting in his room alone in the Dark". Rya whispered.

Stefen Noticed Rya holding Harry's hand. He looked at Harry and Harry lowered his head.

"Do you want to become her brother?" Stefen asked Harry.

Harry looked at her and said "NO".

 Stefen asked "Do you want to marry her?" and smirked.

Harry blushed and said "Yeah." Rya looked at both of them.

Suddenly Dani came and said; "Don't talk to him. He is cursed, he'll bring you death" Harry started to stumble. He turned to go back to his room.

 "Hey, from now on we're best friends. Ok? I don't really like our little princess having another brother. But if you want to marry her then that means we're good. So, let's get along brother" Stefen said with a warm smile.

 Harry looked at him with a sweet gesture. This is the first time someone called him brother, this is the first time someone ignored

Dani's harsh words and someone talked to him like this, this is the first time someone called him best friend. He burst with tears and this is the first time he cried because of happiness.

Everyone looked at Stefen surprisingly.

Sam walked to Harry and held him to stop him crying. "I wanted to say those things before Stefen, but he stole it. So, can you also take me as your best friend and brother? I'll be your confrere; you prince of the Dark world." Sam said and smiled at Harry.

Prince, really; he never heard anyone called him that other than curse, he never felt he even belonged to the Dark world. Harry couldn't ask more than this. This is all he needs.

He got a family; he got something he could ever ask for. He suddenly realizes that but this won't last. What about their family? Did they let them be friends with him? He was lost in thoughts.

The maid came to them and said the feast was ready and invited them. Rya dragged Harry by holding his hand to the main hall. That time he realizes; he never wants to leave her side and always wants to hold her hands.

Watching all this, Dani busted with jealousy.

(Main Hall of the Dark' Palace)

"What the hell are you doing in the main area Harry?" Cyrus the Dark king shouted.

Harry couldn't say anything. Ade the peace king noticed Rya holding Harry's hand.

He asked "Did you become friends with him?" They looked at each other and said yes without looking at their parents.

The peace king laughed and said "That's a good thing to hear about children. I'm happy for you all." They all looked so happy.

Stefen added "Dad, I did make him not only my friend; he is going to be my soul brother, in fact he'll be my only brother" Stefen said so proudly.

"And dad you know what, I'm going to be his confrere. Just like how you like Harry's father. You said even though you belong to the magic world and brother to uncle Rex, you have always been the side of Uncle Axel; Harry's father and you both are best friends. I'll be like that to Harry from now on" Sam said to them and giggled.

His father, Magic duke; Henry wipes his tears and says "I'm so proud of you my boy".

The Dark king busted with anger.

He shouted again "Harry, you go into your room" Harry frightened.

The magic King Rex interfered. "Harry, do you like your new friends?" he asked.

"Of course, they're the only friends I've got. And I like them with my life." He said in a shivered voice.

"I think you don't have to let him live alone anymore Cyrus. Let them choose their lives, what they want to become. In fact, it's not in our hands. It's already written. We can't change anything about how much we tried to protect them. At last, it's their story, not ours." Rex the magic king added.

He walked towards the kids; he can see Rya still holding Harry's hand. "So, do you decide what is he to you? Stefen and Sam already said theirs" he asked Rya.

She looked at Harry and her father and said; "I don't know, but I think I don't want to lose him" she doubtfully said. The magic king patted both of Rya's and Harry's head and said to Harry,

"We're your father's friends. He is a great man. Sorry for not being there for you when you are having your hardest time, but you're always welcome into both magic and peace and consider it as your family." King Rex said to Harry softly.

They all eat together that day. As for Harry he felt alive from that day on.

[Years have passed, Rya becomes 19 and the boys become 21].

Rya becomes the most beautiful and powerful in the entire universe.

She started to look like a bright sun. Even her mind, heart and soul are as bright and strong as she is. She always carries her sword along with her. A golden sword, slim and having a silver, golden and black stone, it's known as the 'sword of universe'. It's the most powerful sword in The Universe; which can cut through and tear any evilest soul and only wield by her. The unique magic she uses known as Golden lightning.

Harry becomes powerful and handsome as a night sky. And his soul and heart and mind glow as a moon and become strong as the powerful night. As like everyone, Harry also has a powerful sword along with him. A black slim and sharp and most powerful among the Dark world named as black demon. His unique magic is known as black thunder.

Sam becomes also powerful with them; everyone calls him a powerful knight of The Universe. His mind, heart and soul shine like a golden star. His sword is the golden shield, which can't be cut by any weapons and magic. It is so powerful; it is slim and golden with green stone. His magic is known as golden blast.

Stefen becomes as powerful as the boys, his soul, heart and mind are pure, clear, bright and known as the White Knight. He shines as a silver star. His sword is known as the balance sword. It can make you judge yourself; your action when it's cut through you. His magic is known as silver strike.

(A lake area on the hill top, having beautiful trees and flowers around it. That is a little far from the three palaces. That's the meeting place for them. They called it heaven.)

Sam is the one always who always came first; he flew from the sky and landed in there with his brown winged wolf. He can see far from there in the sky Stefen is coming with his white unicorn. From the first day they met they declared that they're rivals.

They both want the title as Rya's brother all alone. They always find a way to quarrel with each other and it is only a simple reason. As some legends say; 'you'll keep fighting. Because you're afraid, unless you don't fight; you may fall in love with each other. That's why love is twisted and different, yet so beautiful.' Just like that they can't live without seeing each other, but when they do, they'll start to fight.

When Stefen comes soon after there comes Rya from the sky with her golden fire phoenix bird. They all waited for Harry to join them. A little late, but also Harry joins them too on his black dragon.

Dani usually doesn't hang out with them. In fact, they also don't like Dani being arrogant and non-humbly, also when he gets a chance, he starts to bully Harry and he doesn't hesitate to hurt him. Didn't value each other and he even didn't like being with Stefen or Sam.

Even hanging out with them is the only reason he wants to win over Rya and become the king of the universe, and always greedy for more power.

"It's so nice to be here," Harry said, staring at the lake. They all looked at him. They also felt he was right. Because being here with each other, that's only what they could ask for.

"Let's build a castle down here, and when the times come when we are up to power, let's live there together." Stefen said with a calm and excited voice. Rya smiled back at him. She never really asked for anything, all she wanted was the wishes they have granted and be with them until the end.

"Want to race?" Sam asked. They all looked at each other and smirked. They got on their spiritual animal and flew to the top of the sky like the wind. All over The Universe can hear their laughs through the clouds. The Universe became bright as much as their happiness.

Where All Went It Wrong

[A bright morning]

They all summoned to the main hall of the magic palace. As usual Harry is the last person who came in there. When he comes, he can see the main hall is filled with some elders of each world and the kings and most of the royals except Sam's, Stefen's and Rya's parents. There is also their dearest big mother; she is the greatest witch of the Trio World who prophesied about their birth and destiny. There is also Stefen, Sam and Dani. They were all waiting for him. He can also see his uncle and most of the elders are pissed to see him there. He just entered the room. Stefen called him by hand gesture to come and sit with him. He smiled and sat there.

An elder stood and said; "why do we have him here? He didn't deserve to sit here with us" all started to murmuring.

Sam got up and said "He is also a prince in Trio World like us. He also deserves to sit here with us." He got really angry. Stefen holds Sam's hand to calm down.

Cyrus the Dark king mockingly said "you all speak for him until you all get killed; or do you have any secret plan to conquer the world with him? After all you'll not get the throne like him!" The elders started to judge and mocked him. Harry couldn't bear them making fun of Sam.

He got angry. "If you have any problem with me, then talk about it with me. Don't put it on others" he said angrily.

"Wow, you got angry, you arrogant little thing. How dare you?" Cyrus screamed. Stefen gets up and spoke

"Don't speak to him like that. He's also one of us. Don't treat him like a slave. He is the prince of the Dark world, so Sam and Stefen couldn't control his anger either.

"How dare you command me like that? I'm the King of the Dark world?" Cyrus screamed and started to curse.

Rya showed up. The whole room shakes in her anger. She took out her sword and leashed forward

"How dare you speak to them like that in front of me? If anyone spoke to my brothers or Harry like that; I Ryana Golden Crown the child of the universe and the Queen, is reminding you, I'll not hesitate to leash this sword through your soul. Don't you; don't you dare to talk like this to any one of them and I shall not show you any mercy."

The Dark king burned in anger and insult. The hall turned silent. Most of them hesitate to breathe.

They all know Rya is the strongest among them; she is twice as strong thrice than the strongest elder in there.

Stefen and Sam looked at her worriedly and she winked at them and smiled. She holds Harry's hand to remind that it'll be fine. Harry again feels so blessed to get them around him.

Big Mother gets up and says, "If you're done, let me tell you what I came here to say."

They all felt so bad. Rya slightly bowed and asked for forgiveness, as did Harry and Stefen and Sam.

She smiled at them.

She continued to speak: "As you all know it's time for the heirs to take power now. They are at their age and also, I saw a terrible future for our worlds. The Dark shadow will take over our universe. Blood will spill and gods will die. That's what I'm saying. Someone who is going to boost the power of Dark shadows will be the god of them." before she couldn't complete the hall became a mess with murmuring.

"What's the point of the young ones taking over the power? Let us fight with them, " Cyrus mocked. The elders also agreed.

"They may be powerful, but what do they know about war?" an elder asked. They started to argue. The heirs sat there saying nothing, they were worried about the future of the universe.

"Let me finish. You're right, they don't have much knowledge about war but they're powerful. They only have thirty-fifth percent of their power. In other words, they are really stronger than the seventy-fifth percentage now." Everyone wondered.

She continued "their original power is only obtained after the ritual. It must happen as soon as possible. The knowledge in the war is not going to save this time. The power they hold alone can save this world. But the ritual, it's so important without any failures. The queen must wear the crown by The Universe directly with her companions' and her king. No time for us to hesitate. Because what's coming is going to put us all in the Dark hole, which is that we'll never be able to wake up or get endless sleep."

When she stopped everyone remained silent. Because this time they got what she meant. What she prophesied happened without any mistakes all over these years.

Everyone is lost in endless thoughts and plans. Stefen asked suddenly: "Big mother, where's our parents? Why aren't they here today?" She said a little worriedly.

"They went to visit the late Dark king and queen's grave." Harry raised his head and looked at her and asked

"Why?"

She replied "All these years, you all are protected by that king and his queen's big sacrificial magic. Yes, Harry, your father and mother being a shield to you all these years, not only to you but for your friends too. At the very last moment they are able to build a shield for it, destroying half of the strength of the Dark shadows. That's why you all are alive today. But now that shield is disappearing. It's time to get you too powerful and protect everyone. The Kings and queens are headed there to strengthen that shield as much as they can, until the ritual day." She said in a comforting voice.

Harry looked so proud of his parents. So, Rya and Sam and Stefen. They thanked Harry by smiling. But the present Dark king burned in anger.

The meeting is over. All are worried about what the future holds except Cyrus the Dark king; he was planning something evil.

Dani looked at Rya; he knew it's time to she chooses her king. He always waited for the day he became the king and ruled the world. He always heals over Rya, but above that he wants to become the king.

Harry, Stefen, Rya and Sam were hanging out in the courtyard of the magic palace discussing what big mother said. "My kids' big mother came to them to speak directly and alone.

"Big mother" they greeted her.

"What I'm going to say, hear it carefully. From now on your magic will start to fade at an edge you feel weak. It's ok, because it's a part of getting ready to accept your pure energy and power. But you have to be careful until the day of the ritual. If the enemies know you're weak, they'll never hesitate to destroy you. So, keep this between yourselves. Warn Dani too." They all look at each other.

Losing power isn't something they worry about. They agreed even though they've so many things running through their minds.

Big mother continued "Rya my beloved child, it's time you've to choose your king. Let's prepare the ritual for the day that comes after the third day from today. I'll talk to your parents. Prepare yourselves. Always be together and be together in the ritual." She said and pats everyone's head.

She looked at Rya and smiled and said "Choose your king and everything wisely. Ask your heart and soul. Don't let anything come over!" Then she turned to Harry and asked him to accompany her to the gate.

When they reached the gate, the big mother stopped and looked at Harry "Harry my dear boy, if you have to choose between this universe and the beloved ones, what would you choose?" Harry looked surprised. He doesn't have an answer.

He looked at big mother without any answers. He said "I don't know. I think I'll…" Before he finishes big mother interfere

"Remember you're born to become the king of The Universe. Also, you'll become the reason for the destruction of The Universe. Protect them, bring the light back from the shadows. Rise when you are down. When the times come don't hesitate to give up what you hold…."

She looked at the sky and before she vanished her tears from eyes dropped at; she whispered "I hope The Universe gave you the strength and happiness my children." She vanished in the wind.

[The other side Rya, Sam and Stefen]

Stefen and Sam were staring at Rya.

Rya felt annoyed and asked "What're you two staring at?" They mockingly said "So it's time to choose the king huh? So, who it is?" They started to laugh.

"Why so funny?" Rya pouted. "We knew it was Harry. Isn't it?" Stefen asked.

"Who knows? I can even choose between you two. Also, there is Dani. Come on, he is going to become the Dark king" she said as fun and laughed.

Sam said "It's not a funny little princess." She smiled and spoke

"If it's not Harry then who is it? My heart and soul only belong to him. My every heartbeat is only for him since the day I met him." She blushed.

Hearing such beautiful words, Stefen and Sam felt so happy.

"Why did Harry not come back? Let me check" Stefen left immediately.

They knew only in this universe Stefen could find Harry so easily. They make fun of them called 'Soul Brothers'. But they always admired their bond.

Sam screamed to Stefen "bring him into 'our heaven'." Stefen nodded.

[Outside]

Harry is wondering about what big mother said. Stefen approached him.

"Lost in thoughts?" Stefen asked. Harry noticed Stefen.

He smiled.

"Come on brother, they both are waiting for you to join. They asked me to bring you to 'our heaven'. Should I start to call you brother-in-law?" Stefen laughed.

Harry smacked Stefen's head and said nothing. But he can read Harry is worried.

Stefen put his hands around Harry's shoulder and asked

"Are you worried about whom Rya is going to choose?" Harry looked at him and shook his head. Stefen looked at him "Then why are you upset?" Stefen worried.

"Nothing, I'm just tired. Let's go back." Harry also put his hand through Stefen's shoulder and smiled.

(Lake area)

They all sit there and find peace in it.

Rya suddenly asked "Hey let's build our Castle here soon and do the ritual there. What do you think?" she seemed so happy to ask that.

Everyone is so excited to hear that. It's their dream to build a castle and live together. They all agreed so happily.

"What do we call it?" Stefen asked.

"Let's name it……" Rya lost in thoughts.

"Let's name it after we built it." Harry suggested. They all agreed to that.

As their dream they build a big and beautiful castle in 'their heaven'.

For the next day's everyone is busy preparing for the great ceremony.

[Next day, magic world]

The Magic king Rex, is sitting in his own throne, taking care of the preparation for the ceremony. The Dark king Cyrus came to visit him.

"Good morning my great friend" Cyrus greeted.

Rex also greeted him and asked to have a seat.

"I came here today for a proposal" Cyrus started the conversation.

"What proposal?" Rex wondered.

"Yes. My son; the future king of Dark World Daniel Blackstone and the future queen your daughter Ryana Golden Crown; what do you call Magic king?" Cyrus asked.

The Magic king patiently said "It's all up to my daughter. It's her right to choose her king. I don't care who she chose. So please let things go as planned. We don't have to force them or anything. That's what I'm thinking"

"I almost figured you would say this. I want to talk to your daughter too. Is she here?" Cyrus asked ignorantly.

"Unfortunately, she is not here. She'll come soon, I guess. She and the children are gone to visit their new castle across the lake" the king Rex said calmly.

"I'll wait until then" Cyrus gets up from his chair and walks to the door.

[The new Castle]

It looks so delicate and dignified. Roofs and walls are gold and silver. Black pillars. It's a castle that would sparkle even in the Dark. On the top of hills with a lake view, it's so dreamy to see, Guarded by each of their spiritual animals.

Rya, Sam, Stefen, Harry and Dani were checking their new castle. Everyone is excited because the ceremony is near. They don't care about the fact their magic is getting weaker and for the next two days it'll mostly faint. They go near the throne.

There are five. In the middle; the throne is the biggest and delicate.

"Of course, it's for the queen," Stefen chuckled.

Next to her throne she stared at it and looked at Harry.

Dani interfered. "So that's the king's throne, isn't it? It's not as big as the Queen's."

Sam felt annoyed. "Of course, because even the king's power won't be near as the queen's," he said.

Harry kept silent. They all noticed that. In fact, they all have been worried about it since yesterday.

"What is it Harry? Why've you been quiet lately? What's going on?" Rya worriedly asked.

He looked at her. His eyes were tired but there was also fire. They noticed he's about to burst into tears. Sam asked "what did your big mother say to you yesterday?" Harry shakes his head.

He stares at the thrones and asks.

"If you've to choose between your loved ones and your duty as the protector of the universe, what'll you choose?" They were all shocked by his question.

They don't have any answers to tell him.

Dani said "I'll choose The Universe and I'll rule it. There is no between." They all remained silent.

They knew there was something bothering Harry and only he knew the destruction was starting.

[Later]

Rya and her father were sitting in the main hall of the magic palace and discussing the arrangements. Her father the king already mentions about the talks with the king of the Dark world; that he came and forward a proposal and all that. But her father never forces to take a decision about her life.

Cyrus entered the main hall of the magic world where Rya and the king were sitting. Cyrus looked at them. They greeted each other and the king offered to take a seat.

Cyrus starts to say "You must know why I'm here. Your father must tell you about yesterday. So, what's your decision Ryana? Whom do you choose as your king?" Cyrus asked Rya with a strong voice.

Rya closed her eyes and took a deep breath and said "to be my king, I already chose him ages ago. There's no need forcing me now with this. And also, there's no need to let everyone know about this. In fact, that's what even my big mother asked me."

Cyrus angered. "If you are going to choose that brat who is cursed; you're putting not only your life at risk but also the future of The Universe and every living thing in it. I won't let you choose him. You're not going to choose the Peace world's prince then choose my son the prince of the Dark world and the future king. Harry that boy only brings despair and destruction to everyone. He is walking death." Cyrus angrily said.

The fact that Harry is hearing everything at the door, he got flustered. The things he heard were the exact things he was saying to himself. He knew it's better he got away from their life. The words of big mother rings in his ears like a warning. He vanished from there.

"He is also the prince of the Dark world. Harry is the son of the true king of the Dark world. Yes, you are right; I'm going to choose Harry no matter what. Don't speak evil about the king of the Universe anymore. This all time I let you do whatever is; you are the one who raised Harry and you are my friend's father. And you're a dignified world's king. So, keep your respect for yourself." Rya couldn't stand when he spoke about Harry like that. She burst in anger and said to Cyrus.

Cyrus who is not satisfied with the situation and the behavior he left there angrily. They already knew he was going to do something beyond their expectations.

Cyrus directly went to Dani and beat him as much as anger he had for everyone. He keeps saying to Dani "your useless brat…" Dani, who has idea what's going on, begged to stop beating him and say what he did wrong. His mother ran in there and grabbed Cyrus's hand and begged to stop beating their son.

Cyrus angrily said "That arrogant girl chooses that brat Harry as her king. What the hell were you doing all these years? I told you to be the one she chooses. Now it's Harry, all the efforts I took these years were wasted. You're useless. I'm going to kill you stupid." Cyrus angrily said to Dani.

Dani felt desperate. "What did you say? How can she choose a loser like him? All this time I was dreaming about becoming the king." Dani said he has no soul in him anymore. Cyrus raised his hands to hit again Dani grabbed his hands and pushed him.

He laughed like an evil. "Why didn't she choose me? I was dreaming to rule the world along with her." He talks like a madman.

"Stop acting like a mad dog. Let's kill that brat Harry now and let it over with. Go and find him and quit acting like a fool." Cyrus screamed at Dani.

Dani laughed again and looked at his father. "I'm going to kill all of them at once. Stop telling what to do. You are useless as a dad. No not really! If I did kill you right now, I'd become stronger. Isn't my father?

Right now, I'm weak, but if I kill my dear mother and father who is also the king of Dark shadows, I'll be the strongest. Is it father?" Dani screamed again evilly.

Cyrus is shocked by the way he is acting. But before he does anything Dani already killed his mother. He was shocked like there's nothing to do. Dani screamed and went towards Cyrus. But the way Dani acts he already knows he's gone mad and becomes the purest evil. He realized after all; big mother's prophecy is not wrong.

'One of them will kill their parents and become the Shadow king' before he came to reality Dani stabbed his Dark sword to his father's chest, and that time Cyrus suddenly remembered his big brother and he wondered why.

Dani became the ultimate power and became the king of Dark shadows without the awareness of universal power.

[Magic world]

Rya is sitting in her room. Suddenly she felt something strange. Her soul started to shiver. She felt something was not right. She wondered why Harry was not in the palace, where he said he'd come sooner. He is late. Harry is always late, but why is she afraid?

Rya called for her personal maid. A young lady came into her service.

Rya asked her "hey Kate, did Harry come earlier by any chance? Sam and Stefen; are they not back yet?" she replied "I didn't see Lord Harry come. And about the other Prince's they are their own way back. The messenger gave the word." She humbly said.

But the face behind her mask everyone failed to see. She did see Harry come earlier and left because he heard the conversation.

Kate; she was born in the magic world; she was always obsessed with Dark magic and she fell for Harry's charm. Right before Rya summoned her, she is with Dani and planning the evil. He offered her the power and Harry. She has to act on what he says and she agrees.

[Next day]

Stefen and Sam were left together to do a mission a little far. The way back to their worlds, they were blocked by some Dark shadows. Even though the magic was not stronger they fought together and were about to win with whatever they got. But suddenly a hurricane appeared. So strong, they wondered who's that. In the blur of the dust, they see it's none other than Dani. They are always aware that one day he's going to fight them for power. At a glance they knew they're no match for him now.

"Why are you doing this? For power?" Sam asked Dani. "Of course, today I'm going to kill you both," Dani said laughing evilly. "How can you become so strong? What did you do?" Stefen asked nervously. Because the way he acts and the power he holds, it's not natural. "I just killed my parents. Now I'm the strongest. I'm the shadow king" Dani said without any guilt.

They fought for a long time. Sam and Stefen were at their limit. A sudden attack from Dani towards Stefen, Sam stands in front of him and dodges. But unfortunately, Sam got that hit really bad. That time they knew there's no escape from this. Sam falls on the ground. Stefen ran into him. Sam knew he couldn't go long anymore. "Go, escape from here. Let Rya and Harry know about him. There's no time for me. So, save yourself." Sam said to Stefen. Stefen looked so shocked. How did he leave Sam and save himself? It's Sam, Stefen flustered.

"I can't. How can I leave behind you Sam? I am not going without you. If we have to die, then let's die together. I can't leave you… I can't. I can't live without you…. Sam, I…." Stefen said shatteringly. He can't even imagine a life without Sam.

Sam holds Stefen's hand and says "You think I want to die. You think I want you to leave me. Look at the situation Stefen, we have no choice. I do want to live in our new castle with our little princess being the Queen and Harry being the King. I want to live with you in that castle. I want to fight with you; I want to be with you. But we have to make sacrifices. We're born to protect this, Universe. I'm going to give you my remaining magic, so you'll be there safely. Don't hesitate. As long as my magic lives in you my spirit will remain in this universe. So, save The Universe. Be the hero…"

Stefen hated the situation, that he couldn't do anything. He burst into tears, he grabbed Sam's face and said "come back to me, I don't care how many years it'll take. I'll always wait for you. You've to promise me that you'll come back and be with me" Sam smiled with tears rolling on his face.

"I promise then. I'm glad Stefen…." they saw Danny aiming another shot at Stefen, Sam suddenly gave his remaining magic into Stefen's. Stefen is ready to go back even though he didn't want to. He looked at Dani angrily, like when the time's come, you'll certainly pay for this sin certainly.

He looked at Sam and closed his eyes. His tears were flowing through his face.

Dani knew when Stefen got there with this, he'd get into trouble. He knew that if he gets strong, he may lose to Rya. Before fighting with Rya, he has to master his power more. So, he can do now, before Stefen vanishes; to erase his memory; the memory he has about now. He shot a spell for that to erase Stefen's memory, which hit so hard that he forgot about the incidents now and 'his beloved Sam' completely.

Dani walks towards Sam "So you don't want to die, huh? You want to live; I think I'm going to make that wish come true. Live as my puppet and see them all fall…." Dani said those and did the spell.

Right after that Sam becomes a puppet who has no soul and heart left in him. He doesn't know who he is, he doesn't remember anyone. There's no emotion left in him. Dani laughed knowing he's about to win and seeing them all in misery.

Broken Dreams

The moon is about to go back and the sun is ready to come back.

Harry goes to a Dark Forest from everyone, hoping no one finds him. He has no idea what's going on around him. Only he knows that he's going to destroy the Universe. The gods will die. He knew the gods were Rya, Stefen and Sam. Only he causes the destruction, and that is what he misunderstood. He doesn't know he already lost one of his beloved brothers. He looked at the sky and wondered they're doing alright.

Rya is waiting for them to show up. She got warned by her mother to not go outside today. Tomorrow it's the ritual. She is eagerly waiting for the day to live in a castle with them. She doesn't want anything, not this power, not this position. All she wants is to live with her beloved ones.

Kate already got the command to take care of Stefen from Dani. "Don't let him go near to Rya" that's the command she got.

Before she notices Stefen is already in that castle and about to meet Rya. But she did so perfectly that she gave him a sleeping potion. Stefen drinks without any hesitation, because she is the personal maid of Rya, who has been with her for years now. And also, he didn't know there were any dangers. She brings him into his room and informs Rya that Lord Stefen is back and Lord Sam already left.

"They said they were really trying to meet you today so they'll meet tomorrow."

"Are they okay? Did you see them?" Rya asked desperately.

"Yes, they're fine!" Kate replied. Rya felt relaxed after hearing that they're okay.

"What about Harry? He didn't come?" Rya asked sadly.

"No words from him. I think they all will meet you tomorrow. Now it's time to take a rest." Kate acted so innocently and left the room.

Rya looked at the sky and said "I hope. Tomorrow is a big day. My one and only dream is going to be fulfilled. But why do I feel so empty?

Why am I hesitating? Why don't I feel happy? Why do I feel something is not right? Is it because they're not with me? I hope everything will be alright." She speaks to the moon and there are tears in her eyes, she wonders why.

The big day, it's the ritual day. The whole universe is excited.

[The new castle]

Rya is waiting for others to show up. Everything is ready and everyone is there, except Harry, Stefen, Sam and Dani. She saw Stefen was approaching.

"Are you alright? Where are Harry and Sam? Did you see them?" Rya asked Stefen.

"Harry, I didn't see him after I got back here. Sam?" Stefen got confused.

Kate suddenly interfered. "Big mother is asking for you."

Rya held Stefen's hand and spoke. "Come with me. Don't go anywhere." She felt that something was off.

"Let's start the ritual. It's getting late. I'm afraid everything is out of our hands. So, let's start with this…." Big mother said to them.

They don't want to do the ritual without the others, but there is no option so they let the big mother decide.

The ritual starts. Rya and Stefen keep looking at the gate hoping they'll reach there soon. Suddenly the atmosphere got really Dark and lots of Dark shadows showed up at the castle entry.

The ritual got disturbed. Big mother warned them not to engage in fights without completing the rituals.

But the numbers of Dark shadows were increasing and more that the three worlds couldn't hold it. They all are down. Even the kings and queens have to surrender, the sight of their parents failing; they couldn't sit there ignoring it. The ritual won't complete without them shouldn't show up.

Rya had no choice but to fight. Their magic gets a little more powerful because of the power of ritual. They fight with all they got. They didn't hesitate when the number of Dark shadows was increasing.

Suddenly Rya stood there shockingly. The one who is leading is her Beloved brother Sam. he is in the front line. She shattered.

He is Sam but what happened to him, she wondered.

Stefen is not hesitating. Why? She looked at him. He looks like he didn't even know Sam. She knew something was wrong. She realized Stefen forgot about Sam already and Sam is not in his own control.

He is more like a puppet, like someone is controlling him. She couldn't bear the sight of her brothers fighting like enemies. She always saw them fighting, but this is different. They were trying to kill each other.

Sam who doesn't know; who're all these ones and Stefen who doesn't know who Sam is and thinks he is one of the enemies.

Rya ran into the middle of their fight. She stood between them. "Wake up, you both. Who did this to you? What happened? Why are you fighting like this? Don't do this. I won't let you kill each other. Please.... stop" She cried loudly.

Suddenly a voice came in. "Crying out loud won't save you now, Rya. Open your eyes, you've lost. Now come to me, I'll show you mercy to not kill you and I'll let you become my queen...." An evilly laugh. Rya stood there shockingly. She recognized that voice; it's Dani. She's smart enough to read the situation by then. She knew becoming weak now will destroy The Universe. She collects the courage to fight the war.

There are so many shadows coming toward them, she has to fight to protect The Universe. She summoned her sword.

She pushed Sam away from Stefen. She knew speaking to him is no use, he's totally lost himself.

She grabbed Stefen's hand and said "He is not an enemy. Don't try to kill him. Dodge his attack to save you. Don't you try to kill him. We're in a war. We've to win" Rya said to Stefen with a fire in eyes but tears flowing face. He understood that everything is a mess now.

He also recognized that voice. He knew that's something off, but it's not the time to think and explain. They're in the middle of a war. He looked around. Most of the strongest among them almost fall. He looked at Sam, he was fighting against them. He saw him aiming his shots against Stefen. Stefen tried to dodge every attack and didn't aim any shots against Sam.

Rya is fighting with her sword. She's still strong enough to summon her sword and fight with it. Dani feels frustrated. He knew as long as she holds that sword, he can't conquer Trio World. Rya fights with no hesitation, only an aim to protect The Universe and her beloved ones. She glared at Stefen and Sam.

Stefen is perfectly dodging every attack like he already knew his movements. Sam is aiming at most every attack against Stefen. She feels so angry against Dani.

 She screamed "Dani.... If you're brave enough, come by yourself and fight with me. Don't hide like a coward." She flows like lightning in the battle field, most of the shadows are down with her attack. Dani feared in her anger.

She hoped in her mind "Harry, are you all, right? Where are you?"

 Not far in a Dark Forest Harry felt something was dangerous going on. He suddenly gets up and gets out of that forest. He rushed to their castle, but he got blocked by a large group of Dark shadows. He fights against most of them. But his current state is so weak. He felt betrayed. He hoped everyone was alright.

Suddenly Dani's voice came "You all surrender now. You're not going to win against me now. Surrender and I'll show you mercy." 'Dani'; Harry was shocked to know the betrayer. He thought of him as his brother even though he always hates Harry.

Harry senses the situation in the battlefield of the castle. Stefen and Sam in a situation like that Harry couldn't forgive Dani. He screamed "Dani, stop this nonsense. I know that you want me, take me and leave them out of it. If anything happened to any one of them, I'll never forgive you" Dani laughed loudly. "Who wants your forgiveness? You're going to die anyway now. They'll die with you too" he laughed again. In his laughs even the devil gets frightened.

A Dark shadow came towards and attacked Stefen in the middle. Stefen got really wounded and couldn't fight with his power. He fights as much as he can and he stands there helplessly.

Rya ran into Stefen to help him, but before she catches him there's another strike through him. Even though Sam can save Stefen, he stood there as a puppet. Stefen falls into Sam's arms. Rya feels Stefen's heartbeat. But the Dark shadows are aiming against him. She knew she couldn't make it in time.

She screamed and begged Sam "Sam, Wake up…. It's your Stefen; it's your beloved Stefen. Please save him. Save him…." she cried loudly. But the next attack also happened and Stefen died in his beloved Sam's arms.

"Stefen……No…. don't die please, don't die please…." Rya screamed and cried. Harry on the other side couldn't hold the enemies anymore and now knowing his beloved brother is gone, he felt in anger and rage.

Sam holds Stefen's body like he is holding something precious. He couldn't let go of him, but he stood there like he had no mercy. He didn't cry. He didn't feel sorry but he couldn't let go of his beloved Stefen.

Rya fights with her rage and anger "Dani…. I'll kill you. I'll make your death miserable. You'll ask for my brothers' forgiveness. I'll make you do it." She screamed.

Harry already fell and he couldn't fight anymore. The Dark shadows captured him. Dani's voice rises again;

"Rya, I'm going kill Harry next. But this time I'm going to give you an option. Remember Harry asked the other day; would you choose your beloved ones or The Universe. Drop your sword and surrender The Universe to me, I'll spare Harry's life. 'Do it." Rya couldn't do anything.

She loves Harry the most. But she was born to protect The Universe. If she surrenders The Universe to Dani, it'll destroy it with Darkness. She closed her eyes and held the sword tightly. She felt like her breath was getting heavier. Her eyes burst with tears. Her body dried without hope. "So, what's your answer?" Dani asked.

"I…. I'm sorry Harry. Forgive me…." she cried loudly.

Harry already knew she would choose The Universe.

"I love you, Rya. I'm glad I could meet you." he said with a smile and tears in his eyes.

"Dani.... I'm not done with you. 'I'll bring you down to the ground and haunt you at the very last, I'll make you wish 'if you were never born'." Harry said with rage and anger and fell to the ground without his breath.

Rya kneeled there. Losing every hope, she has lost her beloved ones.

Sam is still holding Stefen, without any reaction and on the other side Harry is also gone.

She knows there's no meaning to life anymore. The more she felt guilty and rageful. Even though she could have them, she stood there pathetically. Having all the power, being the strongest, she failed to protect her love.

In her state Dani took advantage and spread his Dark shadow all over the over The Universe. The Universe starts to get Darker.

Rya took her sword and stabbed herself. "Dani... this is not the end. I'll be the one who'll take your life."

She sacrificed herself to give the light to The Universe and protect it. Her magic spread all over The Universe like a light and as a shield. She made a shield for the Trio World to protect it. As long as the shield remains, Dani could never touch those worlds. As long as he doesn't conquer the Trio World, he'll never become the king of the universe. She falls to the ground remembering all the good memories with her loved ones.

She saw their dreams were shattered by their castle turning into dust without them.

"This is not what we have in our dreams, right? Father, mother forgive me, I'm not able to be a better daughter for neither you nor a better queen for The Universe. Forgive me that I let you down. Stefen, Sam I am so happy to have you two as brothers, if The Universe have mercy and give me another life I want to be born again as your dear sister. Harry forgives me; I love you too and you're my only king. I lost my heart with you. I wish I could choose you...." her eyes closed and fell into a hole of Darkness.

The Dark shadow took over The Universe. Blood has spilled and gods died. Someone takes over the power of Dark shadows and becomes the god of them.

The Universe felt alone. The Dark shadows danced in the Darkness. But they didn't know that the light will come back and they've to disappear from The Universe for once and all

Different World

Rya startled and woke up. She looked around. She touched herself to check. Yeah, she's alive; she was brought back to another life. She is reincarnated.

She saw Stefen lying on the other bed next to her. She ran to him. She holds his hand and touches his face. Stefen is alive. Her tears fall from her eyes. She calls him. "Stefen, wake up...." she sniffled.

"He's just unconscious. Don't worry, he'll awake soon" Harry came into the room. As soon as she heard his sound, she felt her heart fall down from her chest.

"Har.... Harry..." even her voice couldn't come out. "Welcome back, Rya" and smiled at her and spoke. She ran into him and hugged him. She holds him tightly.

"I'm sorry. Forgive me...." she cried loudly. He holds her face and told

"You did nothing wrong. You don't have to be sorry. I've always loved you anyway!" she blushed and put her head on his chest. They both felt comfort while holding each other.

"Where is Sam?" Rya asked.

"He left" Harry said sadly.

"Left? Why?" she asked.

"He said he'll come back" he doesn't have any answer to give her.

She looked at Stefen. "Can you look after him? I'll be back" she told him.

"Yeah" he nodded. He knows what she's going to do. "Go and bring him back." Harry said to Rya. She nodded. She closed her eyes. She's a bit confused about whether she can use magic now or not. Harry patted her shoulder to give her strength. She felt courage.

She vanished right in second.

She appeared on the roof of a huge building where she could see the whole town.

She saw that it's almost dawn. She looked around. She saw Sam sitting on the edge. Rya walked into him.

She called him "Sam…" her voice was breaking. He turned with teary eyes.

He didn't have the courage to look at her. He got up and looked at her.

"Rya…" he called her with a shivering voice. She holds him tightly.

"I'm sorry brother, I couldn't save you…" she cried loudly as her guilt flowed in her tears.

"I'm the one who is sorry. I was greedy, I'm still. That's why I'm still holding you all, after doing everything like this…"

They both cried in their arms and let their hearts feel a little comfort. "Let's go to where we live now. Once we're together, let's figure out everything together." Rya said to Sam.

"I can't Rya. I can't…" Sam said with a low voice.

"Why? Is it because Dani? Are you still in control of him?" Rya worriedly asked.

Sam shakes his head and says "no, I'm not in his control anymore. But I don't think I can come with you." "Why?" Rya asked.

"I don't think I can face Stefen after he remembers everything about me. I let him die in my arms, the one who told me he'll wait for me however time it takes. He told me to come back to him, and I let him die in my own arms. I didn't try to save him, instead I tried to kill him. I can't face him Rya…" Sam said with a heart broken voice.

Rya held Sam's hand and said, "He told you to come back and it's time for you to come back. Even he can't understand you, then who will get you Sam?" If you feel guilty, this time protect him whatever you got just like I'm going to do " Rya's words felt like a comfort for him.

Even though he has hesitations he said he'll go with Rya. "I promise this time I won't let anyone hurt you." Rya promised to them in her heart.

Rya came back to their mansion with Sam. Harry is waiting for Stefen to wake up. When Harry sees Sam, he goes and hugs him and smiles heartily.

A while later Stefen opened his eyes. He lies there for a moment. He looked around, he saw Rya sitting next to him. She almost fell asleep. He touched her hair. She woke up.

"Stefen…" she called him with a warm smile and teary eyes. He smiled back at her back. He's still in denial. He doesn't say a word.

Harry came into the room. When he saw Stefen sitting in his bed he ran into him and hugged him tightly. They hugged each other, patted and smiled.

Suddenly Stefen saw Sam at the door. His smile faded. Rya and Harry looked so nervous.

Sam called "Stefen…."

"Who're you exactly?" Stefen asked Sam and it broke his heart.

"You don't remember him?" Rya asked in a broken voice.

"I only remember him as Dani's puppet. That day he brings the army straight to the castle. That's all I remember…but…but" Stefen said and grabbed his head with pain.

They understand that Stefen is in pain. Rya looked at both Stefen and Sam with a guilty and sorry face. Sam stood there saying anything.

Harry held Stefen's face and said "it's ok. It's ok, you'll remember him. I promise…. He'll be here with us. You have enough time. So don't stress out. Just take a rest."

Rya looked at Harry. He told her to come outside. He also brings Sam.

"I think Stefen still can't remember Sam, because of Dani's damn magic. He's trying to figure it out by himself. But I think it can't help?" Harry said to them. "We can cure him by our magic, only he can trigger the exact memories of Sam by him. But how can he?" Rya asked.

"We'll find a way. Let's give him time. We can assure that he still wants to remember Sam as Sam, not just a puppet." Harry said, looking at Sam.

They can see the moon is brighter that day even on that Darkest night.

[Morning]

Sam is sitting on the couch, Rya lying on Sam's lap. He's patting her head while looking at Rya's and Stefen's childhood pictures. Stefen came to the hall. When he saw them both, he stood there a little.

Harry suddenly called Stefen in a low voice.

He flinched. "What the hell are you doing?" Stefen asked desperately. Harry laughed.

"What are you peeking at?" Harry asked.

"Didn't you see them? Your girl is lying on another man's lap, don't you get jealous?" Stefen asked Harry.

"Why would I? That's her brother. Do you think I'll get jealous by this? He is like you to her. And I'm really happy seeing her resting like that without worries." Harry said and looked at Stefen.

"Brother, like me?" Stefen asked curiously.

"Unless …. Are you jealous that you're not the one who is lying on his lap?" Harry asked sarcastically.

"What?" Stefen flinched. "I'm jealous that she has another brother now and I'm not the one she chooses to rely on," he said loudly.

Harry laughed.

"This whole time she's relying on you. Now let them be. He deserves it, Stefen." Harry said while looking at them.

Stefen felt something when Harry said that. His head plays images instantly that he can't even process. But he knew Sam is someone they all hold dearly; someone they love more like a family. No he's family; he said to himself.

"And also, it's not a competition brother…" Harry said to Stefen and laughed. Stefen remembers the same words when he saw Harry when they met Jay. He slaps Harry funnily.

They both laughed.

Rya and Sam looked at them. "What're they doing?" Sam asked.

"Ooh let them be. They're still the same. The soul brothers…" she said unbothered. Sam looked at them affectionately.

Rya felt grieved for Sam. Rya got up and sat. She called Stefen and Harry to sit with them. They sat there on the couch together. Stefen stared at Sam. Sam awkwardly smiled at him.

"Do you sleep well?" Stefen asked Rya.

"Yeah, after a long time…" she replied with a smile.

"Don't you have any nightmares today?" Harry asked.

"No. in fact that's not just nightmares after all. They were the memories that engraved in my soul." She said and smiled again. Her smile is enough to make their day.

"Does anyone feel Dani's magic's presence around? Because since yesterday I didn't feel like he's around." Rya asked everyone. They both agreed.

"If he's around it's time he came and threatened by now. Since he knew we got our memories and power back, he won't stay back" Harry said.

"When we find him, let's kill him right away. No need for any explanation." Stefen said angrily.

Rya shook her head and disappointedly said "The thing is I can't feel Trio World too."

"You're right. Why can't we feel Trio World? Where is it?" Stefen panicked.

"Only Dani can answer it. We've to find him and ask him. With our current magic we can't find Trio World, since it's so powerful. Our body can't even manage our spiritual power more than this. If we want to cultivate, only little by little. Otherwise, this body will shatter…" Rya said to Stefen.

He asked worriedly, "You think he already captured Trio World and obtained its power?" Harry interfered.

"I don't think so. Because, if he did, the world would already be in Darkness. But it's not. That's mean…." Rya looked at Sam.

"Why don't you say something? Do you know anything?" Rya asked Sam.

He looked at Harry.

"Dani is still searching for the Trio World. He still can't find it." Sam said to them.

"What do you mean?" Rya asked shockingly. They all looked shocked.

"The day you all went; Trio World went missing. There is no trace of it." Sam continued. They all were worriedly looking at each other.

"Trio World is gone missing? How was it even possible?" Rya murmured. "Is that why we were reborn to find Trio World again?" Stefen shared his worries.

Rya looked shattered. She flinched in fear. They all worriedly looked at her.

"What is Rya?" Harry asked worriedly.

"You all are forgetting something. Without the Trio World this universe can't go on. If Dani can't find Trio World these three hundreds of years, do you expect we can find it soon? This universe will shatter. Every living thing will become dust." Rya desperately said. Rya looked at Sam.

"What else do we need to know?" She asked him.

"There is someone, Dani calls him an unknown spirit; he's so powerful. He is the one who protects you all from Dani all these years. He is the one who stops Dani every time he is closer to find Trio World and become the king. He's the one who helps you to hide from Dani. He's the one who also saved me from Dani's control." Sam said with closing his eyes.

"An Unknown spirit, who is it? If we find him, if he helps us, we can find Trio World, right? How do we find him? Do you know him?" Rya asked hesitantly.

"I don't know who he is. No one knows. All these years we all searched for him, but no one saw him except as a fast wind. Only I know is he's so powerful, but he can't kill Dani. He tried so many times. Whenever he kills him, Dani's magic shatters for a while, it may take many days. He'll become vulnerable and powerless. But he'll be back again with cultivating his magic. In this universe, only the universal sword can kill him.... It's your sword, little princess. Only you can kill him." Sam said knowing it's going to make more confusion in their mind.

Harry looked at Rya. When he saw Rya with a woeful face, he felt sharp thorns were piercing in his heart.

[Later at the garden]

Rya is sitting on the chair, thinking about the whole thing. Harry came into her.

"Are you alright?" he asked her.

Rya worriedly said "Yeah, I'm not sure. Don't you feel frustrated after hearing all these? Our world is missing. We don't know how to even find it. Even if we had our magic, our spiritual power is so less. We don't know how much this body can balance the power even if cultivated. If we don't find Trio World soon the whole universe will perish. Our whole lives become a lie. How do we solve this? I still have no idea?" Rya sighed.

Harry didn't say anything, just sat there and kept hearing her.

"And who is this unknown spirit? Why is he helping us? Where did he come from? How did he know about us? It's all bugging me." Rya continued and she looked at Harry.

"Why don't you say anything?" she asked him.

"I missed you, Rya. I missed you so much. I missed the four of us being together." Harry said with a smile. She doesn't have any words to tell him. She hugged him.

She wants to tell him she missed him more than anything. Every night he came to her dreams and disappeared when she woke up, all she asked to see him in person and hold him till the end. But she didn't say anything; all she did was hold him tightly like she only belonged to him.

"Rya, you're the only one for me and always will be. I won't let anything happen to you again. Even if I have to go to the edge I won't hesitate. All I know is I love you. And I will protect you, at any cost." Harry confesses to Rya in a pitiful voice.

She held his face and asked "Harry, is everything alright? Are you hiding anything from me? What are you going to do?" She shows her worries. He shakes his head.

She kissed on his lips and said "you're the only one I ever love. It doesn't matter which life, where or anything. I always love you, Harry. So be with me till the end. Love me like you ever do, even though I don't deserve it...."

She confesses to Harry with tears in her eyes and a smile on her lips. He keeps looking at her eyes and he feels his heart is ripping from his body.

"I'm the one who doesn't deserve you, Rya. But I still love you and I always will. I can't live without you anymore. Please don't leave me…" he cried in her arms like a little kid. She holds him tightly.

[Later]

Sam and Stefen join them eventually and they all sit together in that garden.

"Don't you think this mansion is more likely our castle? They look almost the same…" Rya asked.

"Now you say that, I felt it too…." Stefen said as he agreed.

Both Sam and Harry agreed too. We never got the time to name our castle back then. Even if it's become dust, let's name it now. And when we find our world, let's rebuild it, ok?" Rya suggested.

"That castle is the most beautiful creation of The Universe," Harry said disappointedly.

"Hey don't say that, I'm the most beautiful creature in the universe…." Stefen interfered. They all looked at him awkwardly. "Ok, ok. We four are the most beautiful creatures of The Universe." Stefen suddenly made it right.

"Why don't we call it 'the castle of creatures?" Sam asked with a smile.

They all smiled and agreed, "The castle of Creatures' that's a nice one."

They all talked and laughed in there for a long time to forget their worries even for a little time.

A Door to the Past Memories

Days passed just like that.

They cultivated their power a little by little. They still wonder where Dani vanished suddenly.

Rya lost her sleep thinking how pathetic, that she couldn't do anything. She crawled on her bed every night.

Everyone eventually takes back their spiritual power.

[A fresh morning]

Stefen and Sam and Harry are sitting on the couch.

They were talking while having some drinks. Rya came into the hall and curled up on the other couch. They all looked at her worriedly.

"What's wrong?" Harry asked worriedly.

"I don't know, I don't feel well lately…" She said in a tired voice.

"Rya, how many days you haven't slept?" Stefen asked and patted her head.

"I don't know, I'm not able to sleep. I want to know about what happened to the Trio World…" Rya said desperately.

"Do you want to go back?" Sam asked Rya? Before she could reply Harry also asked

"Don't you like it here?" She can hear both the despair and pain.

She shakes her head. "I like it here. I like wherever we're together. But I want to know our world is alright. I just want to be relieved that it is still the same. I just want to make sure that this universe is alright……" She said in a calm voice.

"What if The Universe finds someone else to replace us? What if they are guarding it already? Maybe the unknown spirit is the one?" Stefen asked curiously.

"Then why did the universe still give our power back? If it's like that, why did our memory come back? The Universe gave our power back for something. And if, like Sam said, only my sword can kill and stop Dani, then how can we find our swords?" Rya wondered.

"I really like it there, you know, I never felt like this at home. Yeah, we're together and it's so wonderful. But being in our world makes me feel at home." Stefen said desperately.

They all looked at each other, didn't say anything. Rya sulked for ruining the moment by her. They all cheered her and shared the drinks and laughed. But deep down in their heart it hurts like it could kill them.

[Later at the university]

They attended the classes as usual and stayed together every time.

They don't want to ruin every moment, whatever the future holds. Every now and then they expect Dani to show up anytime.

Stefen is sitting in the university garden.

The wind softly touches his face and hair. He turned around; he saw Sam was behind him.

"Hey…" Sam nodded.

Stefen smiled at him when he saw suddenly, and wondered why.

"Why are you sitting alone?" Sam asked Stefen.

"I'm waiting for Harry. He'll come by now." Stefen said without looking at him.

Sam saw Harry is coming from the other side,

He said "Oh here he is coming. Then I'll go and check Rya, her class is about to finish. I'll go and bring him. You two just wait here…." Sam left before Stefen could say anything.

The all feeling messed up in his heart, he felt there is a big part of him that is still missing, that he couldn't find till now.

"What's wrong?" Harry reached Stefen and asked.

"I don't know. Brother, could you tell me who Sam is to me. I can't go on like this. Every time he is around it feels like my head and heart is exploding. I know he is a big part of me. I know he is someone special to me. But what exactly is he to me? I want to remember him;

I must remember him...." Stefen said desperately. Harry couldn't control his tears

"I know you're hurting, so is he. And I promise I'll do anything in my power to remember him. But it's only at the right time. And the question you ask, what is he to you? It's a question only you can answer, Brother. But I promise you, this time I won't let anyone take away from you." Harry said, holding Stefen's hand. Watching away from them, Rya and Sam feel so hurt and admire their bond just like always.

"Hey, you're Stefen right?" A girl appeared in front of Stefen and Harry suddenly.

"Yeah, I'm!"

Stefen replied. Harry noticed Rya and Sam were watching them from not that far.

"I'm Emma. I'm from the same branch as you. You must have noticed me."

She approached Stefen. "Sorry my bad, I really didn't notice you really. Is there anything you want me to do for you?" he humbly asked.

"Oh no. It's just that I would like to go out with you. I heard you've no girlfriends. So, if you're ok, we can go out and get some coffee." She said and blushed. Stefen feels so awkward about what to say.

The face he holds made Harry laugh. Stefen noticed she is beautiful.

"I'm sorry. I'm not really thinking about dating right now. I apologize." Stefen said again humbly.

"It's ok; I just want you to know my feelings. That's all. She said to him and awkwardly left without looking at him. He felt guilty.

He called her quickly and said "Let's have some coffee as friends. If it's ok with you" he offers. She nodded happily.

He looked at Harry. Harry is looking at the other side. Stefen also turned there. He saw Rya and Sam. Stefen stared at Sam.

"What're you staring at?" Sam sulked.

"You," Stefen said without hesitation. Rya and Harry looked at each other surprisingly then laughed hard.

The clouds felt alive after a long time. The breezes reminded me of the warmth and love in happiness.

[Mansion]

Rya is lying on the couch while Sam and Harry are looking at the pictures of Rya and Stefen.

Stefen is outside with Emma having their coffee. Rya is looking at the glass ceiling, thoughts running through her mind. A sparkle of light shines through the glass and she raises her hand to touch it.

When the light touches her hand, her Trio mark on her right palm shines. That's when she noticed her marks again. She suddenly jumped from there and screamed "This is it; this is it……" They were both shocked.

"The door, I know how to open the door in my father's office room. Come with me now" She screamed and ran. They follow her. They stand in front of that door.

"See this mark on the door" She pointed to the triangle sign in the middle of the door.

"And now look at this" She shows her triangle sign in her palm.

They realized what she was saying. They told her to try to open the door. She presses her palm on the door according to the triangle sign. As a miracle, it opened. They entered that room.

That room is filled with memories of them. It's their Trio World memories in paintings. They were all shocked. Rya busted with tears of happiness. She looked at Harry and Sam; they're also looking so happy. They take a look at each picture.

Sam noticed a picture of him with Stefen.

'It's painted by Rya on Sam's birthday. Sam demanded that picture to Stefen as a gift from him being together and it is their most favorite picture together.' Sam holds that painting and his tears drop at it.

"What's going on?" Suddenly, Stefen appeared at the door. He walked into the room and looked at each memory once they lived. All in those memories he saw Sam.

He knew Sam is not just some random person in his memory, and when he saw those pictures, his heart felt like it was busted. He notices the painting on Sam's hand; he bought it and looks at it. At the very moment he looked at that painting he felt like his head and heart was going to explode.

He screamed in pain. Harry looked at Rya and they both nodded to each other. They do the spell to remove Dani's curse from Stefen.

Stefen fainted to Sam's arms once again. In this Universe the most he cares about is in his arms once again and this time he holds him tightly and promises to never ever let him go, and the tears flowing on his cheek were a reminder that he is not in anyone's control now.

Stefen opens his eyes. He is in a Dark room with no one around. He got up and walked to the door. He sees Sam at the door and he is walking away. He tried to stop him but Sam is ignoring him. Stefen ran behind him but he vanished in the fog.

Stefen startled and woke up. He looks around, he is still in his bed. He realizes it's just a dream.

Rya ran into him "are you awake? Are you feeling, ok?" she worriedly asked.

Stefen nodded and patted her head to not to worry.

"Sam, where is he?" Stefen asked while running his eyes around the room.

Rya looked at him with hope and asked "You remember now, right?" Stefen smirked and spoke

"He did come back"

"He is in the garden," Rya happily said. He got up from his bed and walked into him.

It's already night. Stefen saw Sam sitting in the garden. Sam sensed Stefen is behind him. He doesn't have the courage to look at him. Stefen came and sat beside him. They didn't talk for a moment.

"Ah, this is so awkward," Stefen said.

"I'm sorry," Sam said with guilt. Stefen looked at Sam, he saw he was guilty.

"You've to be sorry. You know this is your entire fault...." Stefen said to Sam.

Sam nodded and said "I know...." His heart is breaking.

"We should have saved that day together, or if we should have died together. You allowed me to escape alone and bear all this misery on your own. You expect me to forgive you for that. Remember even if it's to live or die, together. You got me? You're not alone anymore...." Stefen said angrily to Sam.

Stefen's tears are bursting with guilt and anger. Sam surprisingly looked at him. He felt that the burden of guilt is finally relieving slowly.

"I'm sorry, you know. I shouldn't leave you that day alone. I forget you. How could I forget you? You're special to me. I shouldn't have and I did.... I'm sorry...." Stefen screamed with all his guilt and regret. Sam hugged him so tightly.

"I'm sorry I'm so greedy to live with you, with you all.... That's why you all have this fate. If I did end there, you'll......." before Sam could finish Stefen stopped him

"Shhh... you did come back. That's all that matters. Now don't let go." Stefen pampered.

"Yeah, I did come back" Sam whispered and hugged him more tightly.

In the sky a silver star and a golden star shine more brightly together.

They both get inside. Rya and Harry are waiting for them to hear, everything sort out beautifully. They all hugged together and laughed.

Rya showed the book they previously found in her father's room. The book is called 'Child of the Universe'. That's really slipped from their mind about it until now. Now they can understand the words and signs in it.

"How did father have all this?" He must know everything about us. "That's why this book and those rooms and everything, right? But how, how is it possible? Or maybe he is an unknown spirit?" Rya asked surprisingly.

"No, he is not that unknown spirit. I know it. He is just a normal human, without any magic power and he is no more. That's the truth!" Sam said suddenly.

"How can you be so sure? How did these all come in here then?" Stefen asked Sam.

"I know! These all are given by the unknown spirit to him. They used strong magic to protect these…" Sam said

"Sam, what is that, you're not telling us? Is there anything we've to know, tell us" Rya said worriedly.

Stefen looked at him also like he was hiding something. Harry looked at Sam worriedly.

"I once met the unknown spirit directly, that day I only saw a side of him. He looked like a beast. He freed me from the chains of Dani. He told me he is searching for you all. When you are reborn, he'll do these kinds of things. He told me he'll find you all and we'll be together once again, so bear it until then….." Sam broke with words. They all looked so shocked and sad at the same time.

Stefen holds Sam's shoulder to comfort. Rya hugged him and said "I'm sorry; you must be so lonely."

"Not really, I've your memories. You know what he told me; Even if the person is not with you or you are not in the same place anymore the memories will not change, it'll be not empty. We can always cherish those memories, and always feel home by just closing your eyes; we can live in those memories. It's enough to live an eternity." Sam said so proudly.

Suddenly Rya and Stefen looked at Harry Shockingly. Harry feared in their glances "what?" he asked them. "Don't you remember, it's the same thing you told us about home? The first day you came to this mansion, remember?" Stefen asked curiously. Rya also nodded and agreed.

"Did you also meet that unknown spirit? Yeah, that may be the words he told you like Sam?" Stefen curiously asks questions.

"I don't remember meeting someone like that. Maybe I will forget him…" Harry replied and smiled.

That smile doesn't convince them.

"Hey sorry, did I also make you remember your old days too. It must be hard for you to live as a slave of Dani. Sorry" Stefen said to Harry guiltily.

Harry looked at them all and said, "We're together and it's all matters now. I don't care how much I've to sacrifice and how much I've to endure, we're together now. We will meet again...." They all smiled at him and hugged.

"Why did that unknown spirit try to find us? What does he get from us? Why didn't he try to find the Trio World, he must know the world will end like that if the Trio World didn't find? Why didn't I try to save The Universe." Stefen asked curiously.

"We can find all the answers only after we find him. Even in this book, someone removed the pages about the future of this universe without Trio World. It's been three hundred years since the Trio World was missing, I don't know how many years it can hold. Let's find a way to find him soon" Rya shared her worries pointing to the book.

"I think he'll find us himself when the time comes." Harry said suddenly. Rya looked at him. She understands something bothering him. She looked worried. Harry patted her head to let her know he is fine.

[On the dining]

"So, how'll we find him? Do you guys have any idea?" Stefen asked like he's still holding on to the previous chats.

Sam looked at Stefen and said "Maybe like Harry said, he'll come and find us himself. Maybe he's just waiting for the right moment!"

"What if he is the bad guy? What if has no intention of saving the world? You think he'll help us?" Rya worriedly suspects.

"I don't care! I decided to stand beside him whatever he's going to do." Sam said loudly.

Harry raised his head and asked "What if he is the villain?" Everyone looks at him. He is on the edge.

"We all lost everything to become the hero. What do we really gain? We stand and watch our loved ones die one by one. And are we going to make the same mistake as it is and going to kill our dears once again; if that makes you a hero what's the point. If he is protecting his loved ones when he can, by all the means it takes. If that makes him a villain then let the world call him a villain!" Sam said and got off from his chair. There is a big silence around them.

"So, you think Dani is also like that?" Stefen asked Sam while Sam was walking.

"No, I will stay by his side for three hundred years. All I can say is he is a pure devil. He never cared about anything except power and position. He never loved anyone now or then. He just slaughters everyone just to get power. He doesn't take revenge, he doesn't want love, he doesn't have anyone around to love him; all he is seeking is the power to rule The Universe. Don't compare Dani with the unknown spirit. It's true, I don't know much about him but I can say that he is also like us, once we lost everything. But now he got a chance to protect his precious ones. And I can understand that. If I've to choose between you and The Universe; there is no between for me. I'll protect you if I've to go against you all."

Sam opened as he could to let them know there is nothing in this universe precious than them and will do anything to protect them. They didn't say anything. They don't have anything to tell. They knew any words were enough to fill the silence. Harry looked at Sam and smiled like he was thanking. Sam stands there without any regrets in his words.

I'm Home!

Rya woke up and walked through the corridor. She saw Stefen is sitting on the couch looking at his phone. She reached to him; she saw that he was looking at a picture where they four together. She smiled and sat next to him. "Oh, you woke up early today?" Stefen asked Rya. "Yeah?" she didn't realize it was early. She saw that Harry and Sam were not there yet. She usually wakes up late. She scrubbed her hair and smiled.

Later Sam and Harry joined them. They all are spacing out. "I'm thirsty. I'll pour some coffee for us!" Rya got up and spoke. "I'll do it" Harry jumped and spoke.

"I'll do it, sit!" Rya sounded like a command. Harry sits right away like an obedient puppy.

Sam and Stefen laughed loudly. Harry never minded it. Rya gives them all coffee and sits next to Sam.

Stefen peeked at them with jealousy. Rya was sitting with him just now and she was sitting next to Sam. The concept of two brothers and sharing Rya is still not acceptable by Stefen still now. But giving the circumstances, he has to be quiet about it.

Harry saw that Stefen is jealous and he wants to tease him for what he did to him right now.

He chuckled and asked "Rya, you must miss Sam all this time, right? You had two brothers and growing up with one makes you miss it, right?" Sam understands what Harry is getting at and decides to join him to tease Stefen.

"Yeah, that must be hard. I'm so sure no one in this world ever takes care of you as much as I do!" Sam commented. "Yeah, I missed you! I always feel like something is missing" Rya cared for Sam and spoke. Stefen looks so worried. He got up and walked into his room.

Stefen sits in his room and thinks about everything they had to go through.

Harry knocked on the door and entered his room. Harry chuckled.

"What?" Stefen ignorantly asked?

"You took it seriously?" Harry asked and smiled.

"Of course, I know I am not a good brother as Sam is. She was never happy with me in the past." Stefen whined.

Harry laughed. "You think? There is no one in the world who could make her happy more than you do; not Sam, not me, anyone. It's you" Harry said admirably.

"Yeah, only in this world anyone can make her sound and safe it's you. The reason she is safe is because she is around you." Sam joined with the conversation.

"I don't think so. You heard she said she missed you this all-time" Stefen whined again to Sam.

"You think I'm not worthy to get missed by her?" Sam asked and looked at him. Stefen feels so guilty by saying all these.

Rya entered the room; knees before Stefen and held his hand. "Without you I'll not be here now. You know it. You were only there for me, as a parent, as a guide and as a best friend. You were not just my brother; you were everything to me. You make me safe and sound. You kept me alive. It's true I missed Sam, but if you were not there, I'm sure I'll be wasted by now for sure...." Rya said, wiping her tears.

He hugged her so tightly and cried. Sam and Harry joined them and hugged together.

"To lighten up the atmosphere, let's sing and dance today!" Harry suggested.

They all agreed and started to celebrate. Soon later that mansion filled with laughs and sound. They all sang loudly and laughed heartily. They lived every second in it.

Rya looked at each of their faces. They are laughing and smiling. She wishes to see that every day in their face.

She remembered when the day she returned into this mansion, she used to say an empty home.

It's so empty at that time but now it's different. Even though there are so many things to figure out, this place is filled with voices, laughs and smiles.

She remembered suddenly what Stefen said; 'Yeah.... then let's make it a home. Our parents will be always watching over us. So, let's show them, the home they made for us is still a home. Even if it feels empty today one day, we will call it a home again. That day this home is full of joy and happiness and my little princess's smile. What do you say?'

Rya smiled and said to Stefen, "I'm Home! Thank you!"

Stefen smiled and sang loudly to let her know his joy. She thanked their parents in this life for having them, kept them safe and gave them happiness.

She closed her eyes and asked to look after them and gave them their blessings. She let her tears go through her cheeks and sent her love to their parents. She kept saying thank you to them.

The Ones We Owe the Most

[A fresh morning at university]

Rya is in her class and she sees at the door Harry and Stefen is waiting for her. She happily got up and ran into them. They walked to the gate behind the university; they saw Sam was already waiting for them. Rya called Sam's name loudly and ran into him loudly. When he saw her like that, he smiled at her and widened his hands to hug her.

"So, what's the plan?" Stefen asked. They all looked at each other. In fact, they don't have any idea what to do anymore. They're ready to face anything when the time comes, right now they want to live with happiness together even if it's for a little time.

"Let's head up to home and think it through," Harry said as a suggestion.

They all agree. They want to be together wherever they are.

[Home]

"You got a new stalker? I saw a boy flirting with you today; he is even changing his subject to get in the same class as you..." Harry said Rya while sipping his coffee.

"Derek? How do you know about that?" Rya asked the suspect. Sam laughed loudly and spoke

"Believe me; Harry is way better at stalking you than you think!" Sam couldn't stop his laughs. Stefen who heard little bit of the conversation jumped into conclusion

"Rya's stalker? Jay?" and Stefen asked.

"No, it's some other guy. Why do you say this to him? She got so many stalkers. You only remembered him?" Harry asked curiously.

Stefen get the feeling that Sam is staring at him from behind

"Look who's talking. You got way more than flirting around you" Rya jealousy murmured. Harry pinched her cheeks and smiled.

"I don't exactly know why I remembered him. But he is the only one who approached her with a beautiful story…." Stefen explained and gulped. For a moment they realized something and looked at each other shockingly.

"How did he know about me and the Trio World?" Rya shockingly asked.

They all looked surprised. "The sacred book" Stefen said something he remembered.

Sam came forward and said "Sit, I'll explain it to you"

They all sat and ready to hear the mystery.

Sam continued "I don't have much idea, but as far as I know that book was written by the unknown spirit. He put a strong magic in that book to keep it safe and the people who protect it. The day Jay told the story; I'm also there with Dani. You remember?" Sam asked.

They nodded.

"That's why Dani wanted to attend the birthday party. I remember he said to Kate 'you think I sit here like a fool? Until that boy is welcomed to his house we can't enter. That book he has is sacred. It contained magic, strong magic. We have to wait until that day and be careful.' So, he waited and entered into that house. But he can't find it. How much he tries he can't find where it goes…." Sam said carefully.

"Then where did it go?" Rya asked curiously. "Don't know. Dani believed finding that book means finding the unknown spirit. That he must know about the danger came from Dani, maybe that's why the unknown spirit moved it from there. I think he was at the party…" Sam explained.

"At the party? So that means we've seen him? He must be there with us. We're just fools who can't find his true identity." Stefen said with anger and regret.

Rya looked so nervous. "We should find Jay as soon as possible!" Rya suggested. "He has moved from this country. Even if we find him there is no use, he only knows what he told us. There is no help there!" Sam said with regrets.

"There're not many people there that day. What if he already left before we arrived?" Harry asked. "Yeah, it's possible too. If he is there that day Dani must find him." Stefen agreed with Harry.

"I don't know! But whatever he is trying to do, I hope he is on the right path." Rya said and sighed.

[Home]

They all are in their own bed rooms. Suddenly the calling bell rang. Harry is the one who opened the door. It was Mr. Rein. Harry looked at him carefully, he saw him in Rya's and Stefen's pictures.

He recognized that man and asked him to have a seat. Harry called out the others. Stefen came quickly. He greeted him.

"Is this your friend?" Mr. Rein asked while pointing at Harry.

"Yeah, more like a brother," Stefen answered.

Harry smiled at them and tried to walk into his room. But Rya came and blocked him and asked to be there.

He respected her choice. She also goes and greets her uncle.

Sam came downstairs too. He saw that man recognized instantly. Mr. Rein also looked at Sam and recognized him suddenly.

"It's you?" he asked Sam suddenly. Sam smiled and walked towards them. So, they remembered things now?" Mr. Rein asked Sam.

Rya and Stefen sat there clueless. Sam nodded. Harry gets up and walks to get drinks for Mr. Rein.

"You did send away the maids, do you?" he asked to Rya and Stefen.

Stefen answered "It's not safe for them to stay here!"

"So, you did remember who you really are! I'm so glad" Mr. Rein said and they looked surprised.

"I know you've so many questions in your mind. I'm here to check on you but I think it's time to answer your question" he said with a long breath.

"Our parents, we knew they knew about us. Do you know details about that?" Rya asked, shaking her voice.

She is so moved that the people around her know everything and keep them safe without selflessness.

Mr. Rein tells the story at once.

"Julie was born as princess and your Ruth was born in an ordinary family [Rya's parents]. Mia was born in an ordinary family and Finn is Julie's brother [Stefen's parents].

We all met in high school. Julie and Ruth fall in love and Finn falls in love with Mia. They were always against the ideas about poor and rich. They really didn't care about the consequences from this relationship.

They joined this university together. I was not as brave as them to go stand against my family and follow my heart, so I moved from here before higher education. But our friendship stayed just as they were. That's why they trust me with their child right?" He wiped his tears and continued.

"They were living together in a small guest house. Soon after the university, they got married. I was not there; even though I was invited I couldn't make it.

One day I got a letter, it's saying Mia was given birth to a boy. And Julie was pregnant too. I was so excited that my friends became parents, I ran into them as soon as I got the letter. When I saw them, Mia's and Finn's child was more than one year old and Julie was about six months. We had a very beautiful time that day. That's the first time they ask me a favor like this. To build a house like the plan they gave me.

I was so surprised but also glad about that decision. I felt something bothering them. I decided to stay with them for a while to help them as much as I can. I built that home as soon as possible and started to live there.

It's that day I knew there was something wrong. There is huge thunder and lightning in the sky. It felt like the earth was shaking. Julie cried loud out of pain.

She screamed like she was on fire. That was so horrible even now to imagine. Mia runs and takes Stefen and holds him tightly like if don't, someone will take him from her. After not long someone in a black cloak appeared and cured her. I didn't see him but I knew he was not something like a human.

He gave a book to her and asked her to hold it until something like this happens. He goes upstairs and I wait for a long time for him to come down, but that's when I realize he just vanished from there. It's not something I could understand.

I waited to ask them till they calmed down. But before that they came to me and told me everything.

Your past; who you really are, how you lived, how did you die and now you are reincarnating. It's hard for me to believe. I heard it like a story. I asked them how they all did. They said the man in black cloak told them.

I warned them not to believe in him, but they refused and said they had these dreams and the things happening just like now is enough to believe in him. I was so mad that they believed in this bullshit. They told me the child to be born is a girl.

I remember what Ruth told me 'She'll bear nothing like us. I and Julie have white skin, brown hair, green and brown eyes but our daughter is going to look like a sun; golden hair, golden skin and golden eyes. Before Stefen was born that man told us how Stefen is going to be and he is exactly like that. You'll believe the day our goddess was born. I was not ready to accept what I heard or I'm so afraid to believe in them. I don't know, I was ready to leave my friends again.

I told them when the child was born and I wanted to be there with my friends. I leave them with so many questions in my mind.

Months after I was informed that Julie gave birth to a beautiful girl. I ran into them and I was so shocked. That child is really looking like the Sun.

Julie's condition was so weak.

She said not to worry, even though she is crying while holding her child. That's when again that man in the cloak appeared and held her hand. She looks fine after that.

He said something to them secretly. They all thanked him. He disappeared just like that again. They didn't stay much longer in hospital; they soon got home with their child. I don't know what is going on but I thought I should help them as much as I can.

The very next day they called me and asked me something, that's when I knew I'm about to lose my friends. They don't live much longer.

Julie was about to die yesterday but that man gave her a little longer time against fate to make her wish come true; to stay with her child a little longer. As it goes for Mia, Finn and Ruth. But their time started to count down. The Man called Dani who was still alive from that time; who was the reason for your death will hunt you and kill again, so I've protected you and brought you two with me till you two demand to come back to here.

I promised them, I will do it and protect you two even if I've to sacrifice my life. I stayed more days with them and left to ask if anything was needed. I visited them sometimes after that.

And the day I last saw them they already left from here. My best friends are important to me more than anything laid there like that day. After the rituals, I saw you two crying while holding each other. I remembered the promise I gave to my friends.

I tried to reach them. That's when suddenly a man appeared in front of you and ran to you like a mad dog. I didn't know who he was, but I assumed he must be a man called Dani. Before he reached you two, that man in cloak appeared and engaged in a fight with him.

I stood there like what to do, that's when he came; grabbed you two, gave it to me and asked to go as soon as possible, he said while pointing Sam. They all looked at Sam.

"I don't remember much but that man in a cloak appeared in front of me suddenly and did something like magic to you two and said to me it'll keep you safe for a time being.

And he asked me to take care of you two. I looked at him through the cloak, I was shocked when I saw his face; he looks like a beast. Before I knew it, in a blink I appeared in my home."

Your parents never dreamed of anything until you were born.

I remembered they told me they want you to live as royalty as your past life. That's why they built that home; they said something like a mansion like your castle.

Then the man in the cloak is also the one who told the one to build like that and he placed a secret room with his magic and told to say only Rya can open that. I hope you opened that door and found something hidden there. It must be something precious to keep that safe ...." He said and wiped his tears. Rya and Stefen are also weeping in thoughts of their parents.

"It's our entire fault, if we're never born as their children, they will be alive till now!" Rya said, cursing herself.

"Don't say that! You know what your mother said to me; 'I must have done something good, isn't Rein? That's why I've the fortune to give birth to the queen of the universe. I must be blessed by the heaven of The Universe.'................ So don't even think like that!" Mr. Rein said to Rya and Stefen.

They sat there for a moment in silence.

They introduced Sam and Harry to Mr. Rein again. This time they told them clearly and he understood better.

"Did our parents tell you anything more about the unknown spirit?" Stefen asked Mr. Rein.

"The who?" He didn't understand who Stefen meant.

"That man in a cloak" Stefen cleared him.

"Oh, him, is that what you call him? Did you meet him? I don't remember anything so important they told me about him. I think even they didn't know anything much about him." he replied while thinking.

They just felt like losing that hope too.

He continued suddenly "Yeah, I remember asking Julie how they could trust a man who doesn't even show his face and even if they knew anything about him. You know what she told me;

'I don't know who he is, I don't even know what he looks like. But what I'm sure is, he'll protect our children at any cost and in this universe, no one loves them as much as he does. I can feel his longing for my child, he wants her to be protected and that's what I believe in.'

Rya murmured something. They all looked at her and she shook her head.

Harry holds her hands, he is shaking. She looked at him worriedly. Sam walked from that place to his room; his eyes were filled with tears and fear.

Stefen said anything but sat there like lowering his head. They were hoping the person they're looking for would not be someone they were thinking.

Mr. Rein said his goodbyes and left. They thanked him again and again for everything he did. He gave them his blessing and said hoping to see them again.

They thanked their parents, to the ones they owe the most.

The Return of Darkness

Days passed quickly.

A week later at the university they were sitting on the garden bench all together they noticed the atmosphere changing. The sky gets Dark suddenly, strong wind blows the breezes and it's getting so cold. Everyone's laughs changed into panic. The birds stop their sweet singing and run away to their home.

Rya looked up at the sky and said "He is back." Everyone looked at the sky worriedly.

Rya closed her eyes for a moment and opened. Her eyes are sparkling like the sun. Suddenly that light reached the sky and brought back the sun more brightly.

They looked at her and realized it's no time to worry anymore. Sam stops the wind into little breezes by his hands and Stefen brings back the birds again to sing. Harry saw the people are still worried about the surroundings. He took that fear from their mind and they started to laugh again.

They hope this time they can make it together.

[At night]

Stefen is walking through the corridor and suddenly he feels there is someone at the door.

He goes and checks, but there is no one. He turns and starts to walk; there is a sudden blow coming towards him. He tried to dodge and it came again and again.

Sam is next door; when he heard the sound, he panicked. They together tried to dodge it but suddenly the Dark shadows were coming countless times.

They started to fight this time but a hit came towards Stefen. It's from Dani. It's not a normal Blow to carelessly dodge. Sam pushed Stefen and stood before him. Sam closed his eyes to get hit and leave all this behind. Still, he doesn't want to die. Stefen screams Sam's name and runs towards his name but it's too late for them.

Sam looked at Stefen and said something. It's not that loud, but Stefen's eyes widened with love and regret. He cried loudly.

The blow hit in time but not on Sam's. Someone strikes that hit. Dani is so arrogant that no one can dodge his magic power. He looked at that person angrily.

It's Rya. He got afraid. She looks so powerful and she's angry.

"If you touch any one of my loved ones again, I'll show you any mercy." Rya said fearlessly and her eyes were burning with vengeance.

She hit Dani with her magic; golden lightning.

He fell far away with even one hit by her.

She turned to Sam and said "Don't you dare to die on me!" This time in her eyes there is also regret and pain.

Stefen feels so frustrated and he just went on with his power high. He instantly blows up most of the Dark shadows.

But as Dani was powerful, he summoned more and more shadow to fight along with him.

He screamed loudly "Rya, this is no Trio World. This is not your world. You're not a queen here. No one knows you. You didn't have anything in here. You all got nothing. I'm the king of this world. I've eternal soldiers. Soon after, I'll be the king of The Universe."

Dani said arrogantly and for a moment they all felt powerless. Dani took that moment and struck even more powerful. But again, someone blew his strike; another one that is powerful to strike Dani's hits.

"You are right, this is not Trio World, but; she doesn't need a crown to be a princess, she doesn't have a throne to rule, she doesn't need a king to be the queen. She is the child of the universe. She is as powerful as the Universe as it is." Harry appeared.

Dani felt really jealous and angry that he could bury this world in Darkness. "Well, well my dear brother. How have you been?" Dani asked Harry.

"Better; without you." Harry fought along with his loved ones again and with their power they managed to fight and win the Dark shadows.

Dani angrily asked "Did you find that Unknown spirit?" They didn't answer his question.

"I'm asking you?" They still ignore his existence. Dani felt really annoyed.

"If you're thinking he is trying to save the world, you're wrong. He wants this world to end." Dani said angrily.

This time Rya looked at him and asked "What do you mean?" Dani laughed arrogantly and spoke

"You are still the Same Rya. You didn't care about you, your prestige or your loved ones, when it came to protecting the world." He laughed arrogantly.

"That makes us both the same. You want this world to be safe as a queen and I want this universe to be the king. We're Same Rya; we're always ready to sacrifice anything for power."

Dani continued. "You're wrong!" Sam stepped up before Dani could complete what he was saying.

"She will do anything to protect The Universe and that's make her the queen. But you, you will do anything to rule The Universe just to become the king. You're not the same" Sam continued.

Dani feels so angry. "How dare you talk to me like this? You were under my control. You think now you're free, you're wrong. No one can erase that magic from you. How much you tried; except he'll do the sacrificial magic." Dani said arrogantly.

"Now he's free!" Harry came forward and stood with Sam and spoke. Dani felt frustrated and turned into Rya.

"If you're thinking he wants to save and protect you along with The Universe, you're mistaken. The unknown spirit, look at this; do you know what it is? It's the page missing from the Trio World's sacrificial book 'The child of Universe'. It clearly mentions the future of The Universe without the Trio word. This universe will perish. All the living will die, except us. We'll remain as a memorial to the world. Do you know why? Only our magic can survive this world. This universe can't survive without more than three hundred years." Dani takes out a piece of paper and speaks.

But Stefen interrupted.

"You're wrong. It's been more than three hundred years now. It's been three hundred years since we're born. So, you're wrong!"

"When you die or I should say; when I kill you all, your magic becomes a shield to The Universe. Now that magic came back to your body, it was absorbed from The Universe. That's what I told you, Rya. You're not in the Trio World and this body of yours is weak. Not just you, all of your body is weak." He laughed arrogantly and continued.

"And that's what the unknown spirit is after. He wants your powers to survive this world. Just think about it if he wants to find the Trio World and save The Universe, it was so easy for him. I should admit it; he is the most dangerous enemy I have fought in my entire life. But he didn't care about saving it, not even finding it. He is so focused on finding you all. Don't you think it's suspicious?"

Dani asked them. "It's more suspicious now you're explaining these all to us. What do you want from us?" Sam asked angrily.

Dani sits on their couch and says "Together, let's find that unknown spirit together and bring him down. You want to save the world by finding the Trio World and I want to catch him and find the Trio World too. We didn't need someone from outside in our fight, right?" Dani arrogantly asked.

"Stand up! Stand up and get out!" Stefen shouted.

"You think we'll join with you; after all what did you do to us? How dare you?" Right now, get out and don't even think about what you just said." Stefen couldn't control his anger.

In his anger the birds cried loudly and the wind becomes colder. Rya stepped up and holds Stefen's hand.

"Don't you hear what he just said now? Get out right now. We want to save this world but we don't need your help to save this world. I'll kill you in the end anyway. So don't get so arrogant. This time I'll protect my loved ones and this universe together. But you'll lose and I'll make you remember everything you did to us." Rya said angrily.

Rya's voice is so fearful and it feels like The Universe is shaking in it. Dani never expected this response from them. He thought they're naïve and they'll knee before him. But he saw the Queen and her companions once again. This time he got really shaken.

He looked at them angrily and said "I'll come back. Don't think it's over. Once I find him, I'll come to you. Just you all wait and see. I'll kill you all again and I'll conquer this world." And he disappeared.

She still doesn't know how to find the unknown spirit and how to save The Universe. But she believes he's around them and he'll come to them himself. If he is a foe or a friend, she decided to face him and Dani and to save the world as long as they're together; but a question remained in her heart; in this war are they really together?

That night Stefen burnt that couch with his magic; the one Dani sat on.

They were so angry and vengeful. They sat around the dining table and thinking about everything. "How dare he is? Does he think that we're a bunch of fools? I can't control my anger." Stefen said loudly and he is so irritated. Sam hold Stefen's hand and said nothing.

"So, what're we going to do now? Do you guys have any idea how things will go from now on?" Rya asked, so lost.

"Things are going to change from now on; that's what I feel...." Harry said desperately.

"Do you all think that the unknown spirit is someone who wants our power and is trying to destroy us? Rya asked disappointedly.

"No! I won't agree with that. He may not care about the Trio World or The Universe. But he does care about you." Sam opposed.

"Yeah, that's right. Remember what uncle Rein said; auntie said he is 'what I'm sure is he'll protect our children at any cost and in this universe, no one loves them as much as he does. I can feel his longing for my child, he wants her to be protected and that's what I believe in.' and I believe in it. What Dani said is not true!" Stefen also strongly believes in him.

"Yeah, I also want to believe in him. After all, I don't feel like he is a stranger. He must be someone we used to know." Rya said she also believes in him. Harry said anything.

Stefen asked him "Why don't you say something? What do you think?"

Harry shook his head and said "He'll protect you whatever happens, that's all I know!" he looked so confident about it.

Sam looked at him and said "Why don't we just live in the moment? We don't know what the future holds, if it's for a moment I just want to be with you all. So, let's forget everything for a moment; after we're still together."

His words are right. They still have each other. They're together. If the future didn't give them a chance; all they have is now. They remembered the good old days and the laughter. They agreed with what he said.

Stefen suggested "Let's stay awake this whole night today!" This time his voice has the same spirit as him; innocent and loving. He's willing to forget his anger and grudge and fear; after all he knows the future is not going to give a favor to them. They all agreed. They all talked and enjoyed every second. Their laughs echoed in that hall.

Still in their laughs their heart kept screams; this moment, if it's not going to take away!

Harry looked at all of those. His tears fall from his eyes to the ground. They noticed him. They looked at him worriedly. Before they ask something;

he smiled and said "All I want is this. All I want to see are these smiles…." his tears are still falling but his smile is so bright at the same time. He felt that he was not wrong.

They didn't ask anything to him instead they hug him together and spoke

"No one can love us more than you do!"

The Unknown Spirit!

Days kept passing.

The Dark shadows once again try to take the power back and make destruction. But this time the lights start to break the Darkness once again. They keep fighting the Dark shadows everywhere and anywhere.

One day Rya was fighting the Dark shadows at the university, she saw Jay at the exit gate. She realizes he is leaving. She got rid of the shadows instantly and appeared in front of him suddenly. When he saw Rya, he was startled.

"Oh Rya; for a moment I was just startled. I did look for you in your class, I didn't see you. I saw your brother and Harry were in their class. I am leaving this university." Jay said to Rya as a goodbye.

"I was in the garden. Where were you? I also looked for you many times. Why are you leaving?" Rya asked carefully.

"You do look for me, why? It's, it's my time to leave here!" he answered without any clear sound. She saw some Dark shadows are coming towards them

"Jay; answer me quickly; what happened to that sacred book of yours? Where did it go? Who took it?" Rya asked in a breath to keep watching the Dark shadows come for them. She secretly blows a hit on them.

"Why are you interested in that? It was lost. I don't know where it went. On my birthday we lost it. My grandmother was so broken; but after a few days we got a letter and it said 'The book goes where it comes from. The lifetime of this world is in a countdown. If you and your family want to live till then; leave this place and never come back' I don't know what it was. We really cared about that too. But that night some creepy creatures attacked us. Someone saved us, it's not someone else; the same guy with Dani."

"Sam?" Rya asked shockingly.

"Yeah, he saved us. He said he is doing it because he owes that to the Shine family. But it's for the last time; we've to leave this place. The purpose of our lives ended there. I don't know what he meant by that, but my grandmother got really scared and said to thank the master and God for everything. We left that very night. I lost my grandmother a few days after that. She asked me to never come back here. But I really need my documents to get back, that's why I'm here now. I'm leaving this place." Jay said everything he knew to Rya.

Rya was so shocked and at the same time confused.

She saw there were creatures coming towards her. Her mind went blank. She couldn't think of anything. She wants to attack those creatures, but she didn't want to get exposed before Jay. She wants him to be free from his nightmares after he leaves this place. Before she could think something there was an instant blow. She turned her head and looked 'it's Harry. Harry noticed she's not okay. He ran into her. He saw Jay standing next to her. He reached them.

"Are you alright? He asked Rya.

She nodded her head. Harry turned to Jay.

"I thought you left this place?" Jay got chilled by his question

"I was. I'm here to collect some documents. I'm about to leave. Nice to meet you guys again. Thank you!" Jay says his goodbyes and leaves there.

"What's wrong?" Harry turned to Rya.

"Sam saved Jay from Dark shadows. He kept it from us. Why did he keep it from us? Why did he save him in the first place? He must have his reasons, right? But why did he owe them?" Rya's voice began to shatter.

Harry said nothing but stood there shockingly.

"Sam owes the Shines?" Stefen asked from behind.

Rya explained everything to him. Harry is about to say something but suddenly the sky becomes Dark. They saw the Dark shadows coming countless times.

"Hurry, let's get home. If not, the people will be in danger. They're coming for us." Stefen suggested while fighting them. Rya and Harry both agreed and they disappeared from there and appeared in front of their home.

The shadows fought them there too.

Sam came from inside from their home and started to fight with his loved ones.

Rya looked at him and smiled. Deep inside she knows her big brother loves them more than anything. They managed to fight the shadows and get into their home.

"Why do you owe the shine?" Stefen asked directly to Sam.

"What?" Sam asked shockingly.

"We're not suspecting or blaming you or anything. But you've to tell us why you don't tell us about what you know about shines." Stefen made his words clear. Sam didn't say anything.

"Sam, you know who the unknown spirit is, don't you?" Rya asked Sam brokenly.

"I know who he is. But I don't want to tell you. I'm sorry. I gave him my words; above all of it I don't want to expose him before he did want to come to you himself. Also, what did I owe to Shines, what I owe to him." Sam said to them like he'll protect the unknown spirit whatever.

"So, you're really going against us for that unknown spirit?" Stefen asked Sam to grab his shoulder to let him turn around. Sam doesn't say anything. He keeps his head down. Stefen asked again "Answer me, Sam! Are you really going to keep it from us?" Sam doesn't know what to say and how to look at them. He started to shiver.

"Stop this!" Harry said angrily. They all looked at him shockingly. Sam shakes his head to be calm.

"He'll not go to tell you anything. So, stop impels him. It's not his fault!" Harry said loudly and angrily.

"Then whose fault is it Harry?" Rya asked him calmly.

In her voice they can hear the answer.

"You also know who that unknown spirit is, don't you?" Stefen asked him in the same voice. Harry understands it's the beginning of the end.

"No one's fault it is. It is ……." Before Harry says something there's a strong thunder breaking through their door. They all startled. Whoever is coming is more powerful now.

They looked at the door and saw someone at the door.

'Dani', he does not look like usual, he is more powerful like that day.

"Huh, don't you think I got stronger?" Dani arrogantly asked.

"What did you do?" Rya asked frightens. She knew it's not normal magic. He won't get this unless…

"I just wanted something and set fire on the town. Huh, it must be ten, no hundred, yeah more like it must be hundreds of people. Yeah, just like those four or five places." Dani tells like without hesitation.

He came here after killing thousands of people. They all busted in fear and anger.

"How dare you?" Stefen asked angrily.

"What? You are angry. I just found out who this unknown spirit is. This all time he doesn't let me kill people like this. I thought he was saving people. No, he is stopping me from getting stronger. Every time he keeps interfering with my business. But for some reason he is busy lately. And I wondered why I didn't give him some surprise." Dani said and laughed evilly.

Rya tried to hit him with a blast, but he dodged it. "Didn't I tell you Rya; I'm stronger. I got thousands of innocent people's lives. You can't fight me in here."

Dani sounded like he's so arrogant in his power. Harry gripped his hands to suppress his anger. Dani looked at him and smirked.

"Why don't you say something my dear brother or should I call you the 'Unknown spirit'!" Dani asked and smirked. They all looked at him shockingly.

Harry the unknown spirit! That word keeps ringing in their head. They didn't ask or say anything to him. "You thought you could play hide and seek forever? This time I'll show you how to play!" Dani said arrogantly. Harry kept his head down and didn't look at Rya or Stefen.

"Harry, is this true?" Stefen asked him suddenly. He just stood there and said nothing. "Ha…. rr…. y?" Rya called him brokenly.

"He won't say anything. He knew he was guilty. You know what Harry? I didn't give a damn thing about what you're going to say. I'm going to find the Trio World and will become the King of the Universe. I will make you regret what you did to me." Dani said and smirked.

Harry laughed suddenly. He laughed so evilly and arrogantly. Everyone was shocked by his behavior. More shocked there was fear in all of their eyes.

"You're right! I'm the unknown spirit! The one you all are looking for till now. So, what are you going to do now? Kill me? Enslave me? You're not strong enough to do so. But you can when you become the king of the universe, right? Harry Laughed again loudly and continued. But you can't be the King of the Universe unless you didn't kill the king; which is me!" Harry looked at Dani and smirked arrogantly.

Everyone was shocked.

Rya looked at Harry with a broken face. Her tears rolled down through her cheeks and even if he wanted to wipe those tears away and hold her tightly; he didn't dare to do so.

He looked at her and said "I'm the unknown spirit and I'm the king of the universe. I was deceiving you. This all time I'm lying to you. And he is right about something. Harry pointed to Dani and continued. I don't want you to find the Trio World and I don't care about the world being destroyed. I'm doing against your will and I'm going against you. My goal is something else. Even if that means The Universe will perish, I don't care!" Harry said without any hesitation.

Dani suddenly tried to hit Harry with his power. But Harry easily dodges it and strikes a powerful blast against him.

Dani couldn't dodge it.

"You know how powerful I'm, you've experienced it. All this time I suppress my power to hide the facts, but not anymore. I'll not hesitate to hold back anymore." Harry said to Dani angrily.

Harry turned and looked at Rya and Stefen. They look at him brokenly and hopelessly. He felt like his heart was breaking into pieces. He didn't dare to stay. "Don't get in my way." He said to them while looking away and vanished.

When Harry vanished, Rya couldn't hold her pain anymore.

All the questions in her remain not cleared. "Harryyyyyyyyy" Rya screamed. She kneed on the floor. She felt like her heart could rip out now. She holds her chest in pain. Sam started to follow Harry; Dani blocked him.

"Where did he go?" he asked Sam. Sam pushed him and said angrily "Don't stand in his way. You'll die in the end anyway."

Dani strikes a blast towards Sam and Sam blocks and returns to Dani. It was new to him.

"I'm not your slave anymore Dani. It was long ago. I'm the confrere of the Dark king or I could say the confrere of the king of the universe. You lost a long-ago Dani. In this game, you're no longer part of it. So, get lost. I hide my powers to protect Harry and it's over. I won't hold back anymore." Sam said and turned about to vanish.

"Sam!" Stefen called him suddenly. "I know! I take an oath to be by his side till the end. I want to be with him. I won't let him alone...." Sam said and vanished.

Dani was so shocked hearing all this. He understands if he wants to go against them, he needs a new strategy. Before he left, he was struck by his anger and ashamed.

Rya cried out loudly. Stefen ran into her and held her tightly. She cried in his arms. He cried along with her. It's the first time he cried along with her instead of comforting her. He is also broken as much as she is. He couldn't find the words to comfort her nor him.

"If you follow me, you'll get hated by them too" Harry warned Sam.

"We came this far for this. We knew in the end this was going to happen. Even if it takes all the means…, remember?" Sam asked Harry.

"Yeah, don't hesitate" Harry closed his eyes and spoke. Their tears gave them strength and courage.

Truth Behind the Lies

Stefen knocked on Rya's room's door. He knows she is at her worst now. He called her name to open the door.

She said in a low voice "Come in".

He opened the door and looked at her. She is lying on her bed. She looks like she has no life remaining in her. He sat next to her.

"If I ask you, are you alright, it will be the worst. But can I say something to you?" Stefen asked her if he has the courage to face reality.

She looked at him. When she saw him like that she got up and sat next to him.

"You know what, they both are really idiots. They thought we didn't know that Harry is the one we're looking for until now. I'm sure you also find it out like I did, maybe before me. You're so much smarter than me." Stefen said to her with a little smile and wet eyes.

"You're right! I knew all along that he is an unknown spirit. I thought he would say it himself. I just want to know why'. He didn't care to tell us anything. Don't we deserve to know it? And Sam. He also left us behind. What are we? Are they really not trusting us anymore?" Rya shows her upset.

Stefen smiled and said "You're right. I was so broken when we heard the truth. But what broke me more is they left us behind. They didn't care to give us an explanation. To be honest I didn't expect that. I thought whatever happens we'll be together until the end. Now I don't know how to find them."

Stefen looked at Rya and grabbed her hands and continued "But I'm glad at least we're together." She hugged him and spoke

"Thank you for always being with me." They both felt comfort in each other.

"Do you ever wonder what happened to Harry that day? What made him do this? I thought he was gone that day, I really felt it. But how did he become the Unknown spirit?" Rya asked Stefen.

"I wondered about it too. I think he may not be gone that day. Maybe he was alive at that time. But why did he have to play like this? is it because of Dani? Only he can answer all of it." Stefen shared his worries too.

Rya looked at Stefen and said "I know what to do? I won't let anything happen to this universe and anything happens to any of us. We'll find the truth soon."

The next day Stefen came down stairs he saw someone sitting on the couch from behind.

It's Dani.

Stefen angrily asked "What're you doing here?"

Dani smirked and said "I'm here at the queen's command. Rya was the one who insisted on seeing me."

"He is right! I'm the one who called him." Rya appeared.

"What?" Stefen was shocked.

"He needs our help to find the Trio World and we need the Dark magic" Rya said to Stefen calmly."

This all time we couldn't find Trio World, now what makes you believe that we can find Trio World?" Stefen asked confusedly.

"Harry made you all a coward. He is not helping you to find the Trio World from the start. He is the one who made you fail, as Sam. They looked like idiots. Now if we use my magic along with you both it'll be not that difficult to find it." Dani said to Stefen arrogantly.

"Rya, are you sure about this? Are you going to trust him?" Stefen asked worriedly.

Rya nodded.

"The question is, could I trust you? I will only help you if you promise to find Harry and you will let me be the king, even if that means I have to kill him. It's not new to you Rya; you have removed him from this world to protect The Universe. You did it before; you've to do it again." Dani said and laughed.

Rya looked at him angrily and said "Don't be so arrogant in front of me. Even if I want, I can kill you right now, I can do it. I'm going to help you; to find Harry, that's what the deal is. I won't break my promise. You've to use your magic to find the Trio World instead. If you break the promise, I'll kill you." Dani got scared in her anger. He spoke

anything. "Rya?" Stefen couldn't agree what was going on.

Rya looked at him and said "I've decided. I can't let anything happen to The Universe. Whatever it takes I'll protect it like always."

"Don't think it'll be easy! He is the king now; he is more powerful than you know. It's a challenge, he challenged us." Dani said he knew Harry's strength and still got terrified of him.

"If he is the king, then I'm the queen. I took this as a challenge. I will find the Trio World. He can't stop me." Rya said to Dani. Dani smirked. Stefen stood there brokenly.

Days passed.

Rya and Stefen started to do the chants to find the Trio World and Dani also gave his share of power. But every time they are about to find it, it goes wrong. They knew it was Harry and Sam. but they didn't give up. Rya challenged them to show them who are powerful.

[A night]

Rya is sleeping on the couch after the long hard work. Stefen came and put a blanket on her. He looked at her pity. He knows she is suffering more than anyone. He really doesn't know how to comfort her or what to tell her. He can only be with her until the end, whatever she decides. He patted her head and kissed her forehead to wish good night.

He turned and saw a movement at the window. He walked to there and spoke

"I know you're here Harry. Listen brother, don't make her sad anymore. I know all along you're the unknown spirit, so is Rya. We can talk it through. You know why I find out your secret, it's not because I'm not smart enough to. Because I knew you brother, all this time I knew you were suffering inside. I really wanted to comfort you. I'm just waiting for the moment you tell me the truth. I know you brother; we have been soul brothers for every life. Why do you leave us behind?

Don't you trust us or because you think I'm useless? Which is it brother?" Stefen asked with a broken voice. His voice started to break.

The other side of the window Harry engraved in the guilty and left with his tears dripping there.

The next day Rya and Stefen wake up sensing a big trouble. Rya gets up from that couch to find Stefen. She saw Stefen standing outside looking at the sky.

She ran into him and asked "What's going on?" in a terrified voice.

He pointed to the sky in fear. She looked at the sky and grabbed Stefen's arms. The sky is getting Darker and it is whirling. They looked at it and they felt like the sky would cover the whole world and everyone and everything in it would perish. Soon a whirlwind also joins the sky.

The atmosphere is getting more dangerous. They both looked at each other and vanished and appeared near the sky. They both tried to hold the disaster as they could.

Suddenly they saw someone also joined them. It's Dark and windy, but I realized it's Sam. They together somehow stop it; and realize it's just the start of the ending.

Sam was about to go back and Rya blocked him. "Where're you going? Don't you see what happened just now? You are still going to erase Trio World and let this happen to The Universe? Even if it is, why do you bother to save the world?" Rya asked Sam to stand up in front of him.

"I never intended to destroy The Universe. But saving Trio World is only a way to protect it, I'll stand against it." Sam replied without looking at them.

"I don't understand what the hell you both are trying to make here? But you both are playing really hard to be the bad guys. And you know what? We'll find the Trio World soon. We won't let anything happen to these worlds. Tell him; tell him we won't let him destroy this world; whatever his reasons are."

Sam left there with a bitter smile without turning back. But before he left, he didn't dare to look at Stefen and Stefen didn't say anything too.

That day Rya felt so frustrated and she felt the urge to find the Trio World on that very day. She looked at Stefen and said "why don't you just say something? We can't let them do anything like this at their will! We've to stop them before they do anything dangerous."

Rya looked at Stefen and continued "I'm speaking to you Stefen; just say something!" Rya's voice gets a little bit louder. Stefen sat there like he's not really there. She realized he's totally broken. She walked to him and patted his head. He suddenly looked at her. His eyes are wet.

Rya sits next to him. "What happened?" she asked him with a pitiful voice.

"Rya, are you sure what happened today is not because of us?" Rya looked at him confusedly.

"The disaster that happened today came for us. Don't you see Sam came to the rescue? He was saving us. Not this world…… I think what happened then and now and what's going to happen is because of us." Stefen continued and looked at her.

She nodded. "I don't know what you are saying? If these are all happening because of us, that's mean…." Before she could complete what, she was saying Dani appeared before them.

"What're you doing here?" Stefen asked angrily. Dani arrogantly smiled and said "You know Rya gave me permission to come here. And we're mates now, Stefen. You can't deny that."

Stefen said with a grudge "I'm not your mate, nor will be." Rya holds his hand to calm down. She knows he's at his limit.

She turned toward Dani and asked "what brings you here?"

"Dani smiled again and arrogantly said "I find out a way to find Trio World with the three worlds' magic." Rya shockingly looked at Stefen and Stefen gave the same look to her.

Rya didn't know how to act now.

All these times she wants to find the Trio World and save The Universe. Now everything has changed. This is not easy. What they think all these times is not true. Harry and Sam are not the real reason why they can't find Trio World, it's them. Every time they close to find Trio World a disaster happens around them. It's because they're finding it. Why? How could they be the reason? All these questions waved in their mind. And they realized they have a long way to go.

Dani snaps them from their thoughts.

"Don't tell me you're going to let them do what they want to. Are you going to let them win? Why are you hesitating? Don't forget they're the ones who left you behind!" he sounded like manipulate.

Stefen looked at him and said "We're not hesitating. Let's do it."

Rya looked at him. She didn't get what emotion was floating in his eyes.

Is it fear? Is it anger? Is it sad? Or is it emptiness?

Dani smirked like an evil. They knew he plotted something more than they knew.

Retrieval of the Trio World

Rya, Stefen and Dani sat together around the symbol of Trio World; a big circle inside a triangle, there's a karma symbol inside the circle and on the left side it's a moon and on the right side it's a sun in it.

They held their hands together and closed their eyes and started to merge their magic.

There were so many obstacles for them to face; by nature, and Dark creatures. They were at their limits but they tried their best to not let go of their hands. Suddenly a huge light came from that triangle where they sat around. They opened their eyes slowly.

They looked at each other happily for a moment without thinking about the consequences before and after.

A little triangle appeared in that light. Rya looked at her palm and realized what to do. She looked at Stefen to make sure they're doing it. He nodded and sighed. Dani keeps smiling like he wins in this war.

Suddenly Harry and Sam came in to stop them.

They screamed 'don't. But Rya looked at Stefen again to let him know, she's doing it and about to touch that triangle by the triangle in her palm. Harry grabbed her from behind by force to stop her but Stefen tried to pull Harry from her.

Sam stops Stefen from doing it. Dani pulls Rya's hand to the light but Harry dodges it. Rya touches the triangle with her and by other hand she grabs Stefen's hand.

Dani realizes the threat so he grabs onto Harry's hand. By connecting to each other by one another the light took them all in it by an instant.

The next thing they realized they're in Trio World.

Rya looked around her, there's no one. She walked through there. All her good and grief memories waves in her mind. Her tears started to drop the way she walked.

She stops her steps when she sees their dream castle in dust. She kneeled there. She screamed in her anger and grief. She felt peace; someone held her shoulder. She looked up. It's Harry.

He tries to help her to get up but Dani interrupts. He knocked his hand from her and stood before her. Harry kicked him and fell far from them.

"You're not allowed to be near her anymore. I'm the one who deserved to be beside her. I helped her to find Trio World, now it's time for you to die by my hands. That's what the deal is between us anyway." Dani said arrogantly and laughed loudly.

Harry looked at Rya brokenly. She didn't look at him.

"I can't die that easily. I didn't no longer desire to live after I lived an eternity. But I don't plan to die by your hands Dani. But if that's what she wanted, I can die for her but before that happens, I'll kill you." Harry said loudly and brokenly and leashed his sword.

Dani also took his sword and leashed and ran towards Harry. But before he reaches, Rya stood there before Harry like a shield.

Suddenly a big golden lighting came.

Sam and Stefen ran toward the place where they saw the lightning.

The next thing they all saw was that she summoned her sword of the universe.

She leashed her sword towards Dani and spoke

"No one touches my man!" her eyes are burning like fire.

Dani screamed at her "You deceived me. You tricked me. How dare you? You dare to break your promise like this? You think you're good to The Universe after doing it?" Dani feels betrayed and he feels shame and anger.

"I promised you only one thing about Harry, to find him. And don't expect me to be a good girl, especially to you after everything you've done." Rya said and smirked.

"He's the one who cheated you. He's one who lied to you, who used. He's eviler than me. He does not deserve to be a part of this universe. He's a devil…" Dani screamed in agony.

"He's, my king! He's everything to me; it's not your concern; if he betrayed me or lied to me and used me. He is my happiness and my sorrow. And his worth to be a part of The Universe is that. I'm the only queen to The Universe and he's the only king for me. I'll not let you speak like this about him and I'll not tolerate you taking another master plan against him. This time you're going to pay for what you did to us" Rya screamed at Dani.

Dani laughed loudly and said to her "Then why don't you just die first then. I know something like this might be happening, that's why I came prepared." He screamed and something like a black fog came out from his chest.

"Rya moves from there. That's Dark shadows commanding fog. If it blasts........." Before Sam's warning finishes a beast jumped over Dani behind Rya.

For a moment Rya got startled. She heard Sam's screams beside her. He ran over to them. Stefen ran over to Rya and made sure she was ok.

"Harry, leave him. Don't do this to yourself. Let us handle this." Sam sounded like begging.

'Harry', that's right. Every time they hear stories about an unknown spirit he is referred to as a beast. They didn't see this form of him.

This is Harry. Rya's tears drop from her eyes when closed her eyes. She can't imagine how much he went through all these years to become like this.

Stefen looked at them and said; "He's not a beast, just looks like a different creature. Isn't it?" Rya opened her eyes and looked at Stefen with admiration.

She replied "Yeah, I wonder what makes them call him that. I can't imagine what it has been these years for him." Rya wiped her tears.

"Yeah, I wonder. Let's not just stand here. Looks like this battle is not going to stop soon." He said while pointing to Dark shadows coming more and more.

"Sam comes here, let her handle them both. We got business here." Stefen sounded like he is all ready to fight how long it takes. Sam looked at them both and jumped and landed near Stefen. They both smirked. Rya saw Harry and Dani are over there.

She reached there and she stabbed her sword on the ground near them. That hit the core of their Dark magic. But even though it's not a direct hit, they didn't completely knock out. They both cried in pain. She felt sorry for hurting Harry but even though she knew it's the only thing he can get out of that misery.

She stabs her sword again on the ground near them, but Harry sees it before it hits him. He throws Dani towards it and he jumps against its dimension.

Dani screamed in his pain, his core of Dark magic and core of Dark shadows came over from his both eyes. Harry jumps over him and grabs that. Dani screamed in pain and anger.

Rya didn't get what's he's doing. But suddenly she realized he's planning to take Dani's power.

He's taking the core of his Dark magic and Dark shadows. If that's what he's doing, all this time it was his strategy; he could take down Dani so easily, but he waited for me to take action to let him out his core. He wants to take away the power over Darkness and to become the ultimate Darkness.

Sam and Stefen looked at him shockingly. First time Stefen felt betrayed by his soul brother. They saw him surrounded by lots of Dark shadows. He screamed loudly. That's the first time they felt him like a beast.

Rya felt numb. She kneeled there, down her head. Her tears didn't come out. She felt a hole inside her heart. Harry didn't look at them. He vanished with the Dark shadows.

The whole world started to shake. Rya didn't move from there. Stefen and Sam run towards her. She didn't look up or face them. She mumbled "Why did he do that?" suddenly a black fog started to spread over there. It's getting Dark and shaky. They felt like they were enchanted in the Darkness. It's got really scary. Dark shadows started to spread all over. It looks like it's the end of the universe. She could hear the screams and cries of people from other worlds.

"Trio World is empty." Rya said and looked at Sam and Stefen.

Stefen confusedly looked at her and asked "What? How did you know?"

I can hear people's screams from other worlds except Trio World. There are no people alive here except us." Rya said and stood up. "

Suddenly The Universe gets more trampling. Sam looked worried and ready to vanish. But Stefen holds his hand and stops him.

"Where are you going? You're still backing him up? Look what he does? The whole universe is about to collapse. You've to be with us. That's the only way we can stop him…." Stefen said angrily.

"Stop him? No one can stop him right now. Even if The Universe came itself, it's not going to stop him. He waited for this for an eternity. He's more powerful than you think. What do you think, he can't take Dani down. He could easily. But even if he did, he can't take the core. So, he waited, waiting for Rya to leash her sword. Even if he wanted to, you can't find the Trio World. He let you find it. Now he's as powerful as you, Rya. But even you can't stop him. Because his will is more powerful." Sam said and sighed.

"His will? What will; is it power or to get stronger or something else? I really don't understand anything. What makes Harry the unknown spirit? How did he become like that?" Rya stepped forward to Sam. in her eyes he can feel the pain yet at the same time the fire of anger.

"Rya, you're right, there is no one in Trio World right now. They have also been erased with Trio World. In other words; you still didn't retrieve these worlds fully. Even if you have to do it, you've to sacrifice something more precious. This won't stand here permanently. This is about to fall soon. The price to save this world is big." Sam said, looking away from them.

"What do you mean, Sam? I don't get it anymore, anything. You're saying all the efforts I took to save this world to The Universe is a waste? Tell me something; is it all happening because of us?" Rya asked.

"Yes, because you took your life. You shouldn't do it. You've to live, yet you took your life. It's your fault; you chose to save this world and he chose to save his world, and I'm standing with him." Sam howled through his pain.

Rya looked at him brokenly. Sam holds her hand and said again

"Forgive me, I'm not blaming you. But you can't blame Harry either...."

Stefen watched all this; he sat on the ground, placed his sword near him and said "It's time you tell us everything Sam. How did he become the unknown spirit? What happened to him? Why is he acting like this? You've to tell us everything right now?"

"I never expect you to be this calm, in a situation like this!" Sam looked at Stefen and spoke.

"I'm. But I'm on the edge now. I'm not going to play along with all this. Say all the things you hide from us or I'm not sure what I'm going to do. Don't test my patients."

Stefen sounded like a command. His eyes are burning with anger. They never saw him like this. He is calm but yet he's so annoyed and angry.

Sam walked towards him and sat in front of him. "There's no need to hide from you now. Everything is already about to end." Sam said and asked to them

"Do you ever wonder how Harry got back to life that day?"

They both looked at him wonder. He turned toward Rya and continued.

"It's you Rya! The one who brought him back to life is you!" Rya stood there shockingly.

The Rise of the Unknown Spirit

'Harry forgives me; I love you too and you're my only king. I lost my heart with you. I wish I could choose you....'

Harry slowly opened his eyes. He remembered everything. The war; he already lost Stefen, he's about to lose Sam. he mumbled "Rya, you're holding on, right?"

He ran to the castle. He doesn't really remember what just happened. He only remembers that the Dark shadows rip his heart. He thought he was dead. Then why, why is he alive now? All these questions lingered in his mind, but the only thing he hoped was to reach his beloved ones as fast as he could. He wishes he could use magic to teleport. But realizes he is too weak to do any magic.

He reached the gate of the castle. There are no Dark shadows around. He wondered why.

He entered the castle. There are his people without breath and unconscious.

He can't think straight. "Rya" he called her in his heart.

Everyone is knocked out. He saw the kings and queens are also down. They are alive. He took a deep breath and felt a little peace and told himself.

"She must be safe. After all she is the strongest"

He walked through there to find her. When he saw her, he ran into her. She was lying on the ground. He took her into his arms. He couldn't breathe, she was not breathing. He tried to calm himself "she must be unconscious. How could she die? She is the strongest." He shakes her to wake her up.

He can't accept the fact that she's gone. He holds her tight towards his chest. He cried out loud, in his grief The Universe started to shake. His teardrops on her cheeks.

Suddenly he got a vision; what happened here and why he is here.

The time she took her life; the most regret is about Harry. If she has a chance, she wants to do it. As for Harry; a Dark world royal blood, Rya's action granted as a sacrifice to bring back Harry. With or without her intention, her guilt, regret and her love towards him bring him back to life.

He burns in anger and grief turns into grudge and anger.

He screamed "Why? Why did you let her die? Is she your child? She is the queen of The Universe? Then why, why did you take her life and keep me alive?" he screamed again and again to the universe.

That's when he saw that; Sam was sitting on the floor, holding Stefen's body. He took Rya and went towards them.

He called Sam his name, he is not responding. Harry realized he is still not in his control. He tried to take Stefen from his arms. But Sam is not ready to let him go.

Harry couldn't control his tears. Sam is not blinking, but yet he's still holding Stefen like something precious to him.

Harry screamed to Sam "Can't you see they are gone. They're gone ……. They are gone…." Harry can't handle the situation anymore. He shakes Sam and screams again "I need you Sam. I need you, so come back to your senses. We can't let this happen…."

Sam's eyes started to flow with tears. He is not moving. Even his eyes are still the same, yet his tears are not stopping.

Harry placed Rya near Stefen and stood up.

He said to The Universe "take what you want from me, and bring back his senses. Bring him back and take me as a sacrifice."

Suddenly thunder hit him and the next moment he turned into a beast.

Sam took a heavy breath suddenly. He saw Stefen in his arms. He is somehow aware of everything till then. He understood why, he senses his soul magic in the Stefen necklace on his chest. He remembered 'As long as my magic lives in you my spirit will remain in this universe.'

The words he said to Stefen and the power he gave him. He kept it, near to his chest. His soul is coming back to him with all the memories.

He cried out loud when he saw Stefen's and Rya's body.

That's when heard a scream more like roar of a beast. He felt like his heart stopped for a moment "Harryyyy…." he ran into the place when he heard the scream.

There's a creature that looks like a beast crawling on the ground through pain.

Sam stopped for a moment. But he saw the eyes of that creature; it shines like Harry's eyes; he couldn't just stand there still. Sam ran into that creature and hugged him and screamed "Harry…., harry…. Thank you. Thank you for bringing me back. But I don't want to see you like this. I'm not worth it, I let them die." Sam cried out loud realizing what Harry was going through.

"I didn't lose myself. I'm glad you're back. I'm glad you're alive" Harry said and howled in his beast form.

Seeing Harry in his beast form made Sam heartbroken. The guilty of losing his beloved ones because of him and now Harry; Sam looked at Harry and asked.

"Am I really worth saving? We lose them because of Me." his head is bowing because of all his guilt and regret.

Harry grabbed his shoulder and said "The day you took me as you brother and conferred; you think I am worth it? Without you three there is nothing left to me in this universe. What happened is not your fault. We can't let this happen; we've to bring them back. We can find a way, till then we've to keep their bodies safe."

Suddenly The Universe started to tremble and shake and a massive wind. They both looked at each other. They ran to look for each and everyone.

Everyone is still unconscious. Sam and Harry looked at each other. They want to save The Universe, but they don't know how to.

"Let's look for a big mother" Harry told to Sam. he nodded and they started to look for her.

They find her inside the castle near the thrones; where the ritual is held. They noticed the ritual was not completed. They felt how Stefen and Rya waited for them to come and join them. Harry hates himself for not being with them in those moments.

"Let's complete the ritual, maybe it'll bring our power back and we can save these worlds and universe" Harry suggested.

"But how; can we do it?" Sam hesitated. Harry nodded and brought Rya and Stefen's body and placed them in their thrones carefully.

"Being by their side, we can do it." Harry brokenly said.

"Yeah, you're right! It looks like they did their performance, now we've to do what we meant to do. I'm glad Rya chooses you as her king already." Sam really doesn't know he deserves to stay by their side anymore. But he doesn't want to leave Harry all alone in this misery. All he can do is be by his side and help him. He knows that's all he can do now.

They sat in their own thrones and started the ritual and somehow completed it. They felt an urge of power filling them. Suddenly Harry changed himself from the beast.

Harry opened his eyes and looked at Rya. If she was alive, how happy would she be now? He couldn't take the pain.

Suddenly the Trio World started to stay calm. The trampling is stopping. The shaking and massive wind is settling down.

They wondered and suddenly noticed something. Rya's and Stefen's body started to shatter like a lightning sparkle. That breaks them down. Harry grabbed their bodies and he's not ready to let go of them.

"Maybe we can find a way to bring them back. But if you take them back, I don't know how to. So please don't take them…." Harry screamed to The Universe.

Sam kneeled and wished for the same as Harry.

Suddenly a formless spiritual voice appeared; "My children, they belong to The Universe. They've to return to their place once and for all. Their body and power shall guide every world here and now. It's the law. No one can break the law; or if you want either way, offer something as powerful as themselves. Unfortunately, there is nothing as powerful as them now. Let them return where they are supposed to be."

Harry couldn't bear the fact there is no way to bring them back. When he looks at them, they're already faded.

"There is something to offer; as powerful as them, the Trio World." Harry said loudly.

Sam was shocked for a moment. "Harry, what're you saying? Without Trio World there is no future for The Universe. Aren't we supposed to protect The Universe, if we sacrifice Trio World for them, this universe will shatter. You're the king Harry!" Sam said brokenly.

"How can I protect The Universe when I'm not supposed to protect the one, I love, how can I be the king when I'm not supposed to protect the one who is always on my side. For me there is nothing more important than you three." Harry said like he already decided to do it.

"You're right Sam, I'm the king and I'm the only one who can sacrifice this world. I'll bring them back no matter what!" Harry continued.

"I; Harryngton Blackstone, the king of Universe, offer you this Trio World and commanding you to bring back the Queen of The Universe and the white knight of The Universe." Harry screamed to The Universe.

Suddenly a big thunder and the Trio World started to collapse.

When Harry opens his eyes, he is in a different world. He understands that the sacrifice is success. But he wonders what happened to the ones in the Trio World.

"I know if you find out what I've done, you'll hate me. But I've to do it, Rya. I'm sorry." He whispered.

He looked for Sam. he walked through that place. He finds a far Sam is also looking for him.

"Where're we?" Sam asked Harry.

"This is the place where normal humans' lives. In this place somewhere they'll be born again. I don't know when, where and how. But we've to find them and we've to protect them. If Dani finds out the fact the Trio World is missing, he'll go mad and will take any means to find that world. If he did that, we can't bring them back." Harry said to Sam.

"So, what're we going to do?" Sam asked Harry to let him know that he's relying on Harry and will follow him.

"We'll stop him; we'll find a way to do it!" Harry said and continued "Sam, do you despise me for what I did?"

"I, Samuele Golden Crown, swear to you, I'll be your confrere and follow you till the end. Even if the world goes against you, I swear you'll never have to fight alone. I'll be the brother and a friend you need as long as I breathe." Sam proudly said.

Harry hugged him tightly and said "Thank you!"

[Days passed]

They both travelled from place to place to find the birth of their dear ones and didn't find anything.

One day they find an urge of atmosphere; it suddenly starts to become Dark and wild.

"Dani," Harry said.

As Harry and Sam Dani is also brought back to this world. His power was weak at that point and now he is stronger.

"Harry, I've got an idea! There is no way he knows you're alive and I'm out of his control. Why don't we take this as a chance?" Sam suggested.

Harry looked at him confusedly.

"I'll pretend like I'm in his control and let's hide the fact that you're alive. We can find his plans and when we find that out, we can easily defeat him."

Harry is not really impressed with that plan because he doesn't want Sam to be Dani's puppet even just for pretending.

"I know you're worried about me. But don't. I can do it and I've to do it." Sam said to him.

Harry nodded and asked "How do you find him?"

"He'll find me himself. But it's time we'll part our ways! I'll find anything and let you know. And when you find anything let me know" Sam said and eventually they said their goodbyes.

"Be careful Sam. I can't lose you too." Harry said and gave a warm hug.

The Rise of the Unknown Spirit-II

[Days, Months and Years passed]

Harry travelled everywhere like a mad man to find them. But he didn't find them. Not only him but even Dani didn't find them.

Sam pretends like a puppet in front of Dani and keeps giving information to Harry.

Harry got stronger through this year's so as Sam. But whenever Harry fought with his power, he started to become a beast. If he changes to the beast it takes many days for him to change back to himself.

All these years Dani never finds out Harry is alive and he never finds out Sam is pretending. He never understands who is intercepting his plans. He never knows who is defeated whenever he is about to find something; someone kills him. And it keeps happening. He scared him, he despises the fact that that man is stronger than him. He named him 'the Unknown Spirit!'

Harry and Sam find some things along the way. 'The Trio World is not gone forever, it's temporarily erased. If the right magic is used, it can be brought back. If it happens Rya and Stefen never will be back. Also, the people in the Trio World are not dead, they are also erased along with that world. They'll be back once the Trio World is back. Also, how many times Harry kills Dani, he will come back after some days with cultivating his power back. only the Universal sword can kill him or in other words only Rya can kill him.'

Harry continued to look for him with the hope he'll find them soon.

"We're destined to find each other. So, I will find you again. Even if I have to set fire all over the world, even if it takes all the means, even if you hate me; I'll bring you back." Harry said day by day.

Sam started to worry about Harry. Harry started to lose control and him. Sam knew the absence of all of them made this way. But he didn't know what to do to help him, but he knew if this continues there is no time until Dani will find Harry is alive and a war will occur again. If that happens Harry would lose his control on himself forever and maybe there is no going back.

One day Harry was walking through a deserted area. The Sun is brighter that day. The Sun Always reminds him of Rya or maybe he never forgets her.

When he walked through, he saw a little boy lying on the sand tiredly. He reached him fast and took him in his arms. He gave him water. When that little boy opened his eyes, Harry asked him "What're you doing in this hot, little boy? Don't you know you'll be dead in this heat?"

"I don't have anywhere to go. My parents died in an accident a few days after I was born. After that my relatives took me but always saying I'm cursed to them all. They never cared about me. A few days ago, they beat me so much and left me in the road. I don't know where to go." that little boy cried loudly.

Somehow Harry saw himself in that boy. If Rya, Stefen and Sam were never there for him, is this how his fate would be?

Harry patted that boy's head, even though he's so tired his eyes are so shiny and it reminds him of Rya and Stefen. He asked "it's okay little boy. What's your name?"

"I don't have a name. They never cared about calling my name. They always call me a little devil and curse." That little boy sniffled.

That breaks Harry's heart. How much pain has this child gone through? "Don't worry; I'll give you a name. Let me see 'Shines'." Harry smiled and spoke.

"Shines?" he curiously asked.

"Yes! I found you on a shiny day, didn't it? Do you want to tag along with me? I don't know where I would go? I may go through so much trouble. But I promise I'll take care of you." Harry asked him.

"What if I bring you bad luck?" that boy asked with a pity face.

"No one can bring bad luck to the devil!" Harry said and looked at that little boy.

He smiled and touched Harry's face and said "if a devil looks this kind, I wonder what an angel looks like?" and he smiled.

"I'll tell you the stories about the real angels on our way!" Harry holds his hands and starts to walk.

Harry told about the Trio World, Rya, Stefen, Sam and him. He told everything to the little boy; Shines and he heard it all like a fairytale. He tags along with Harry wherever he goes. Harry tries to protect him from any harm and he erases all the scariest memories from him.

"Why did you care so much about that boy, Harry?" one day Sam asked Harry.

"He reminds me of myself. You and Rya and Stefen there for me and I want to be there for him now!" Harry answered with a bright face.

Sam felt happy to see aliveness in Harry's face again. Sam also gets along with Shines too.

"What do you think about Harry, Shines?" Sam asked him while let him sit in his lap.

"He said himself he's a devil. But I don't believe it!" Shines answered. "Then what do you think?" Sam asked again.

"A broken angel," he replied.

Sam smiled and asked again "did you like him?" that boy nodded. "Why?" Sam chuckled.

"He always tells me good stories." He smiled and spoke.

"Stories?" Sam curiously asked. "Yeah, about the angels who protect The Universe and sacrificed themselves. There's someone like you in that story too." he whispered.

"Is that so? Then let me tell you a secret. They aren't angels. They're the gods. And they were the reason why these worlds still shine." Sam said with wet eyes.

"Thank you Shines!" Sam continues.

"Why thank me?" he asked

"Never mind," Sam smiled.

When Shines grows up, he eventually understands that the stories he heard were not just fairy tales. It was all true. Shines grew up to be a fine young man and Harry and Sam stayed the same. They never aged and they never changed. Harry kept erasing the spiritual memories with him from his memories.

Harry wrote everything about the Trio World and them in a book and asked Shines to keep it carefully.

"Give it to your next generation and after and after that. Tell them to keep it carefully and precisely. It will keep your family from evil because I put my power in that. I entrust you with that." Harry tells Shines. And he never questioned Harry.

"Why did you do it?" Sam asked Harry.

"When the time comes, they get their memory and power back, they can easily find us. We can't lose a chance. And I want someone to know about them in this world except only us and I want them to be known as the gods who save The Universe." Harry answered.

Shines grow again. He started to live apart from Harry. He got married, became a father then a grandfather.

The last day of Shines he wishes to see Harry and Sam. After a long time, Sam visited him but not Harry. Shines was lying on the bed after losing his health.

"Why didn't he come?" Shines asked.

"He said he can't bear the sight of losing you too. He already endured more than enough. So am I. Losing someone we cared about is not an easy thing to watch" Sam said with a painful voice.

"I came here today to tell you something. Thank you, little boy; for accompanying Harry in his journey and saving him from his misery for a long time. And I promise you, one day I'll repay you for that by protecting your family." Sam continues.

"I saved him? He was the one who saved me and I was always grateful for that. When he took me and took care of me, it was the first time I felt there was someone who cared for me. Now he's grief for the thought of losing me, there is nothing I could ask for in my life. For me he was my father, guardian and God." Shines said with dripping tears and a smile.

And he passed away with that smile.

[Hundreds of years passed again.]

Again, Harry travelled everywhere like a mad man to find them. But he didn't find them. Not only him didn't even Dani find them.

Sam pretends like a puppet in front of Dani and keeps giving information to Harry.

All these years Dani never finds out Harry is alive and he never finds out Sam is pretending. He never understands who is intercepting his plans.

One day Harry called Sam for a meeting.

"What's happening?" Sam asked curiously.

"They're coming back. They were about to be born again in this world!" Harry excitedly tells Sam. they're so happy for the coming back of their loved ones. They didn't want to think about the consequences right now.

"They are about to be born again as a human to the normal humans. I'm going to meet those people and protect them by any means. If Dani finds out and plans anything, inform me right away." Harry continued.

Sam excitedly nodded and at the same time worried.

When Harry was about to leave Sam asked him; "Harry, what about Trio World? Do you find anything to save it? Are you really intending to destroy this Universe? If they find out about what we did, do you think they will forgive us?" Sam asked unintentionally.

Harry looked at Sam and asked "Sam, are you scared? Right now, my only goal is to save the ones I loved and I really don't care about anything else. I know if they find out what I really did, they're going to hate me but like I said I really care about anything even hated by them. I'll bring them back and save them."

"And I'll be right by your side to go through all the way and till the end. I took this oath before and I am still reminding you that you don't have to go alone through anything." Sam reminded Harry that he's still on his side whatever happens.

The Hidden Truths

Time passed.

Harry met Mia, Finn, Ruth and Julie [Rya's and Stefen's parents]. He tells them everything about Rya and Stefen except him and Sam. They're not ready to believe what Harry said but after Stefen's birth they are convinced.

They named them Stefen and Rya as per Harry's Story and also built a beautiful home like their castle with the help of Harry.

Harry knew they couldn't live that long after giving birth to the superhumans; but they wished to live with their kids for a little while more and asked for Harry's help. Harry granted that wish as a token of gratitude. They took care of them as a privilege and as an honor.

Harry calculated that Stefen's not going to remember Sam even after he gets his memory back, that's why he stores those paintings and pictures to remind him. He puts spells and magic to protect that room, especially from Dani.

Dani eventually finds out about Rya's and Stefen's birth.

He planned to kill their parents to get hold of them but Sam informed Harry right away. Harry informed Mia, Finn, Ruth and Julie and asked to be cautious. Even though Harry knew there was not much time for them to live. He also warned them about their situations.

When they know about the attack, they're ready to let go of their lives but they want to save their kids. They informed their dearest friend Rein, who they told everything already and asked him to get their child that very night.

They informed Harry everything and Harry accepted their decisions. They lost their lives and Rein took Rya and Stefen to his home, protected with help of Harry and Sam.

Harry disguised as a reborn in front of Dani by disguised as a child and growing up. It was done by his powerful cultivating and he was succeeding in it.

After all of it, it went perfectly as planned by Harry. Harry defeated Dani every time as the unknown spirit and Dani never found it.

He kills Dani again right before he came to the same university as Stefen and Rya. Even though he knew Dani was going to wake up very soon, he needed some time before that to be with them.

Sam guards them with his longing and guilt and his love.

The night Dani reappeared Rya felt an extreme pain in her soul and heart. She cried for help and Harry understands why it is. So, Harry puts a spell to take a deep sleep. The next day Dani shows up and she knows there is something bad going on, but when she tries to wake up, she feels like she was enchanted. She didn't understand it that time but Harry's magic was holding her to go to sleep. But as powerful as she is, even without any intention she broke that spell easily.

Every time Harry meets Sam secretly and discusses their plans and information.

Seeing Jay was a sudden surprise and a shock to Harry. Hearing 'Shines' reminded him of that little boy. When Jay talked about the sacred book, Harry was so happy that they still carry Shines will and at the same he was shocked and scared. He didn't want anyone to get that book, neither Rya nor Dani. If any one of them gets it, they'll easily find out that he's the unknown spirit.

Sam already informed that Dani was also planning to get that book to find the unknown spirit. He destroyed that book before anyone would get it.

Harry was the one who commanded Jay's family to move on and live secretly. That same day the Dark shadows attacked them by Dani's command. But Sam showed up and saved them and he owes this to their family. He never forgets the promise he gave to the Shines 'to protect his family'.

All these times while pretending, Harry knows; one day they're going to find everything. But until then he wants to live with them and protect them, so does Sam.

Until We Meet Again

Rya falls on her knees, dropping tears unstoppably. She doesn't know what to say and what to do now. She felt like her heart was going to rip down.

Stefen sat there without saying anything. His eyes didn't stop from tears.

All this time Harry and Sam save them and do everything to keep them alive; the thought makes them speechless.

"I really don't know what is planned right now. At that time, I thought Harry wanted to save both you and The Universe. But soon after he realized only one can save, and I know he never cared about The Universe." Sam added.

"I'm sorry! I.... never knew ...what you both went through...." Rya's voice cracked.

"There's nothing to apologize for. But you can't ever blame Harry for any of these. I watched how he went through every day. He lost you and Stefen. Even though I was there with him, I always knew I'm not enough for him as Stefen." Sam said while looking at Stefen.

"I want to see him. I want to ask for his forgiveness. I want to......." Stefen busted in tears.

Suddenly The Universe started to shake strongly. Even they can't afford to stand straight in there.

"We've to stop him. There must be another way!" Rya said to both of them.

"If we've to go and find him, first we've to break this wall," Stefen said and pointed to that black and Dark fog.

That's when they noticed something.

Dani; he is crawling on the ground. They realized he's not dead yet.

Rya reached him. She leashed her sword towards him. Dani was frightened and started to scream "please spare my life. I'll not do anything wrong anymore. Please forgive me. This one time please." Dani begged for mercy.

Rya's eyes were burning with rage and vengeance; she wanted to blame him for everything. "You even spare our parents in this life. They were just humans and pure. Yet you killed them." Rya said angrily.

"They were meant to die anyway. If you blame them for their death, what Harry did was wrong too. He was destroying this universe. He was also bad." Dani said loudly.

"He was bad for a reason!" Stefen defended Harry.

"Unless like you, he was saving someone he loves. What's your intention? To become powerful and stronger? You even killed your parents for it. So don't you dare to compare yourself to Harry?" Stefen burned in anger.

Stefen leashes his sword and says to Rya "Let me kill him, Rya. I want to let him know his actions. He has to die knowing what he's done so far." Stefen pointed his sword towards Dani.

"Please spare me, I promise I regret what I've done. Please…. Sam, you tell them. I apologize for what I've done to you…. please…." Dani screamed. "Stefen……. please………" He begged.

Rya smirked and leaned towards him "remember what I said to you that day. 'I'll make your death miserable. You'll ask for my brothers' forgiveness. I'll make you do it.'

"I won't let you kill me like this…" Dani screamed and tried to raise his sword. Sam stabbed his sword on Dani's hand.

"Dani, I already told you; you were already out of this story. You can't do anything now." Sam said with his vengeance.

Stefen stabbed Dani with his word on his chest with all his rage and vengeance.

When Dani got stabbed by the karmic sword, his life mocked him. 'What if I was good to Harry? What if I was being a good brother to him? Being a good and loyal friend to everyone? What if I changed my father's mind from being evil to good? My mother, the only person loved me unconditionally, yet I killed her. Did she regret being good to me at the end? When I think about it, did I truly love anyone exactly?

Was I good to anyone? Now I see why I can't be like him. Huh, I wonder how this will change my life.'

He can imagine how beautiful it could have been. He stopped his breath slowly and wore a little smile.

The shaking continued. They can see the end very soon.

They started to fight all they have got. This time they were so determined beyond what they can express. The Dark fog slowly started to fade.

"Stefen, you just go and find Harry, only you can find him." Rya said loudly to Stefen while she fought the Dark shadows.

Stefen nodded and left suddenly through that Darkness. Rya and Sam are confident that Stefen can find Harry wherever he hides, such as Stefen.

Not too late Stefen found Harry sitting on a rock in his true form. He remembered Harry left with his beast form, so he was expecting him in that form.

"Harry…." Stefen called him loudly.

Harry didn't turn or look at him. Stefen reached him and shook him. When he touched Stefen can feel the pain inside Harry and how much he endured and faced. He felt Harry screaming inside.

"Harry wakes up…." Stefen shook him again and again but Harry didn't even move a finger or his eyes.

"What's going on?" Rya and Sam showed up.

Stefen looked at them worriedly and said "He isn't responding. Don't worry he's still alive. But there is something wrong." Stefen's voice was shaking.

"No way; don't tell me Harry, this is your plan from the start." Sam shockingly said.

"What's going on?" Rya asked.

"He's……he's sacrificing himself…." Sam's voice started to break.

Rya was shocked. Her eyes widened and the tears filled. But this time she didn't let it fall.

"I won't make the same mistake again. I won't let him die. I won't sacrifice again. Once I choose The Universe and my duty above him. But, not again." Rya said and walked towards him. Even though her heart felt like it was ripping apart. She knew there is no way to save him if he only existed in his soul mind. But she knew it's not the time to be weak. Once being weak makes her lose everything she loves. She said to herself to be strong.

Stefen looked at her walking towards Harry and made that decision, he felt hope too. He looked at Sam and Sam knew what that look meant.

"I won't let Harry die…. If Harry was thinking all this time, then I'm going to stop him." Sam said to them.

"How can we make our moves?" Stefen asked Rya.

"We're going to enter his soul mind." Rya said and sat near Harry.

She holds Harry's hand. Sam and Stefen also joined her. They held their hands together and closed their eyes and started to enchant. It took a moment to enter Harry's soul mind.

They saw a black waving sea inside his soul mind. And they saw he was sitting at the shore looking at that sea.

When they saw him, they ran into him calling his name "Harry" They called him loudly.

He looked at them and smiled. He looked so happy when he saw them. They reached him.

Stefen hugged Harry tightly and said "I'm sorry. I'm so sorry that I didn't get you at that time. Thank you, brother, for saving us all these time…."

Harry hugs him back and smiles again. His smile looks so bright more than they ever saw his smile.

Rya held Harry's hand and said "We know what you are doing. And we know why. But you did enough. Let's find a way together. I'm sure there will be. So please wake up and come back to us. I don't want to lose you again. You think I can live without you? That's why I'm begging don't do this to you." Rya begged.

Harry pulled Rya over him and hugged her tightly. "It's too late. You see, part of me has already faded. I only existed in my soul mind. I won't wake up anymore Rya. Do you think that I will destroy The Universe you protected with your life? I just wanted to bring you back and make you safe. When I found out there is no way to protect you and the Trio World together, I understand I've to give something more powerful. So, I was planning to get Dani's magic cores and be powerful to let myself be the sacrifice. But only you can destroy him. So, I waited for the right time. And the time has come...." Harry said with a little smile.

"I won't let you go alone" Sam stepped up. "I told you; you are not alone in this fight. I will always be by your side no matter what you do. So, if it is necessary for you to die then let me come with you." Sam continued.

"I'm always grateful for you Sam. But you've to live. You've to take care of them both. You've done enough. So just live happily. That's the last thing you can do for me." Harry said to Sam.

"Stefen, I was so happy that day, when I found out that you're going to be born as her brother again. I knew only you can take care of her. So, look after her, when I'm gone." Harry said to Stefen.

"Thank you for the both of you for being a good brother to me, always and forever." Harry said again with a smile and wet eyes.

"It's time for me to leave" Harry stood up.

"No, no. I won't let you leave me. Then take me with you. I don't want to be without you." Rya held him and screamed.

"I told you; I only exist in my soul mind. There is no turning back. You knew it very well. I've to leave soon. I was expecting to see you three one last time. Now I've to leave." Harry said to her.

"You can't. I won't let you. Harry, do you know why I took my own life that day? Because I knew all along, I can't live without you. If I get a chance to go back to that time, I will choose you over and over again; above the trio, above The Universe and above everything. So please I'm begging you, please don't leave me." Rya said again and again.

"I know. I know how much you love me. And I'll always love you more than anything and everything. That's why I'm doing this. I'm glad to die for you. It's not your fault what happened. I want to see you being the Queen of The Universe. So live and be happy." Harry whispered to her.

"Until we meet again" Harry said and hugged her for the last time.

And he faded in her arms.

When they opened their eyes, they were already out of Harry's soul mind.

Harry fell on Rya's lap. She held him and cried loudly.

Sam and Stefen also held them and cried.

"Why? Why did you give me this power? Why did you make me strong if I can't protect the one, I love the most? Why?" Rya screamed to The Universe. "Give him back to me. I don't want any of this power and this position. Just give me my Harry back." Rya screamed loudly again at The Universe.

Suddenly that formless spiritual voice appeared again "My dear child, why are you asking me. Don't you know we share the same power? I'm you and you are me. You've to find how powerful you are. You are not just any queen; you're my child. I don't want to see you broken."

"Bring back Harry. That's all I want." Rya said not hesitantly.

"You can bring him back. Like I told you, know your power and be my child and be the Queen for real. You all fought enough. You all saved every world." that voice gone after saying this.

Rya wiped her tears and closed her eyes. She felt strong waves inside her. She can feel Harry's smile when she closes her eyes. She slowly opened her eyes and touched his face and spoke

"You will come back. You've to. And I'll find you like you find me wherever you're. Until then I'll wait for you, we all will wait for you and the throne of the king waits for you, however long it will take. You shall be known as the bravest who sacrificed his life to save The Universe and everyone will wait for the return of their king. Until we meet again…." Rya said and kissed him on his forehead.

He started to fade like lightning sparkled in her arms.

The Trio World retrieved completely. Everyone looked for each other. They felt like they were in a deep sleep.

[The Trio World]

Everything is back to normal. There are no attacks of Dark shadows. No one dares to use Dark magic. Peace and harmony in every world.

Rya, Stefen and Sam build their dream castle once again. There is no differentiation within the Trio World. Rya became the Queen and Stefen and Sam became her companions. They together take care of The Universe.

Everything became perfect and they all waited for the return of their king who became their hero.

[…………..]

[Years passed]

On a peaceful street

A young boy who looks 21 years old with night black hair; eyes are like black pearl and fair white skin. He looks like a moon at night. He is walking through the corner of that road without causing any inconveniences to anyone.

Suddenly a bully bumped into him. Even though it was not that young boy's fault he said sorry to that and started to walk from there. But that man was picking on him.

That man started to yell at him. When he raised his hand to beat that young boy, suddenly that man's hands dragged behind him and beaten up with a formless unknown. Everyone looked at him terrified.

When he walks through, he feels like there is someone following him. When he turned and looked, he saw no one. So, he walked fast.

When he reached an empty road, he felt like there was someone behind him. He turned and looked again.

This time there is somebody, not just one. There are two young boys who look exactly like his age.

A young boy, he has White silver hair, ocean blue eyes and fair skin. He looks like a Silver Star in the sky and the same old boy with yellowish brown hair, ocean green eyes, and golden skin. He looks like a golden star in the sky. They dressed like kings with shiny clothes and crowns. They smiled at him.

That young boy looked at them weirdly and suddenly he felt there was someone behind. He looked at and saw a beautiful young girl. She has golden shiny hair, golden crystal eyes, golden fair skin. She looks like the sun.

That girl smiled at him and said "Let's go back Harry!"

When she asked, he smiled at them. They flew deep in the sky together.

The stars aligned once again. With the heartily laughs every world cheered and The Universe drowned in the blessed

About the Author

Risvana Hyder

Risvana is a 24-year-old with a master's degree who loves to write. By day, she's a business coordinator, organizing things with precision. But in her free time, she dives into the world of imagination, crafting stories that captivate readers.

Her first book, "The Castle of Creatures," takes you on a magical journey filled with mystery. With every page, you'll be drawn deeper into her fantastical world.

But Rivana's creativity doesn't stop there. She also enjoys writing songs and poems, using her words to express emotions in a way that touches the heart.

www.ingramcontent.com/pod-product-compliance
Lightning Source LLC
LaVergne TN
LVHW041841070526
838199LV00045BA/1390